# CRU

## BOOK ONE OF

# THE
# OGMIOS
---
# DIRECTIVE

# STEVEN SAVILE
# AND STEVE LOCKLEY

Proudly published by Snowbooks

Copyright © 2017 Steven Savile & Steve Lockley

Snowbooks Ltd | email: info@snowbooks.com
www.snowbooks.com.

British Library Cataloguing in Publication Data.
A catalogue record for this book is available from the British Library.

Paperback / softback
ISBN: 978-1-911390-12-1

First published March 2017

Secret Service Mandate 7266, otherwise known as the Ogmios Directive, sanctioned the formation of an elite team under the command of Sir Charles Wyndham. Their orders are to do anything and everything necessary to preserve the sovereignty of the British Isles. What that actually means is difficult to pin down. They are deniable. They act outside the law, removed from the security of the State.

If something went wrong they were on their own.

If something went right no one ever said thank you.

It was enough that when things went to hell, they were there. Sir Charles, known affectionately to his people as the old man, calls them the Forge Team, but their nickname amongst themselves is the Lost Cause.

They serve at the pleasure of Her Majesty and report to a faceless bureaucrat in the upper echelons of government known only as Control, though no one with the power to would ever admit that.

These five men and women are often the last hope.

# ONE

## August 1968

The air was alive with the sounds of death.

Gunfire.

The thunder of tanks rolling into Wenceslas Square.

Yells.

Screams.

Everyone knew that the troops were coming. People had built makeshift barricades across the streets as they opened into the square. Burned out cars and buckled bed frames, and anything else they could scavenge. They were no match for the relentless tanks.

"Wakey wakey, sunshine. Time we weren't here."

Charles Wyndham checked his watch. He'd barely managed a couple of hours of sleep. He felt like crap. It was going to have to be enough.

"Tanks?" he said, as he listened to the twisted dawn chorus in the near darkness of the room. It brought back memories that he'd rather forget. He could smell it out there. Death.

"You might want to take your shoes and socks off and count those little piggies, see if they are all there. Knowing some of our so-called friends, I wouldn't be surprised if they'd nicked half of them to flog while the last little piggy went wee wee wee all the way home from the black market." Paddy O'Dwyer stood at the side of the window so he could look out in the street without being seen from below. The absence of light in the room behind him and the darkness of the street meant he could have pressed himself against the glass and remained virtually invisible, but he wasn't taking any chances.

"Any word from back home on what we're looking at?" Charles asked. If the Russians were moving into the city, it was going to make their lives a whole lot more unpleasant. All they could do was watch and wait. The waiting was the worst part. They had their orders, but they couldn't carry them out without one key piece in the puzzle: the principal. They'd been sent in to help with a defection, making sure the principal was smuggled out from behind the Iron Curtain and back to Blighty to spill the secrets that were being bartered for their liberty.

"Radio silence."

"Marvellous. We should let London know what's going on," Charles said, lacing his shoes.

"Not our concern, soldier."

"What do you mean? Look out there. London needs to know what's going on."

"Absolutely. Couldn't agree more, old bean, but we're not the ones to tell them. Every communication we make increases the risk of discovery. If we blow our cover, we put our people on the ground at risk. It's got to go through the right channels. There are plenty of people feeding information to Control. We stay schtum. Heads down. Don't risk bringing any attention on our people."

Charles knew that he was right. He inclined his head slightly, admitting it. The Irishman was passionate in his beliefs, and he held a lot of them. Somehow, though, he was capable of detaching himself from any situation and looking at it dispassionately. His world was all about results. He got the results London wanted. That made him a valuable piece on the board. Charles didn't agree with his partner's politics, but that didn't mean he wasn't about to learn everything he possibly could from the man, or that he didn't trust him with his life. He did. He absolutely had to. Out here, his partner was the only thing he could count on.

"You still think she'll come?"

"She has to," Paddy said. "Simple as that. If we don't get her out there's no knowing how long she will be trapped here, then it's only a matter of time before someone blows the whistle on her. The clock's already ticking."

"How long do you think we should give her?"

"As long as it takes."

"Meaning until we get pulled?"

"I'm not leaving her behind, Charley. I like you, kid, but here's the deal: I've seen too many people cut adrift and left to sink or swim. I'm not like that. Greta deserves better than that. She deserves a couple of heroes."

Charles didn't feel like a hero.

For one thing, he was scared.

Greta.

That was what this was all about. Or who. Paddy had been even more erratic than usual for the last three days while they had been holed up in the abandoned house, eating tinned meat and dried biscuits washed down with water they had to fetch from a standpipe in the middle of the night. They had been saving three bottles of beer until she came, so

3

they could celebrate their last day in this hellhole together. Not that Charles thought they'd ever get to drink them; the mission had a hoodoo sign hanging over it. He could sense it. Long after they were gone, those three bottles of beer would be left standing on the shelf, gathering dust.

"We might have to," Charles said, fearing the response he might get but knowing that it needed to be said. Paddy had to face up to the possibility that she was not coming. That she might not even be alive. It was the risk that they all took and the fact that she was a woman made no difference at all. If anything, it made it worse.

"Be heroes?" Paddy said. "Every day."

"That's not what I meant."

"I know."

"You think this is just a show of strength? Moscow flexing her muscles?" Paddy said, moving to one side to allow Charles to take a better look at the lie of the land.

"Not a chance. The Great Bear might like the world to think that they have come to keep the peace, to protect the security of their territories, but this has nothing to do with peace. It's expansionism, pure and simple. This is as much about conquest as Hitler's plans were. Instead of the Third Reich, we are witnessing the aggressive and all-pervading spread of communism."

"You know what that sounds like to me, Charley? British colonialism," Paddy jibed, seizing the opportunity to give another dig about the way people were still being treated in his homeland all these years after Oliver Cromwell.

Charles ignored it, as he always did. It was part of the game. There was no point in taking the bait. It was an argument he could never win. "The difference between the Russians and the Nazis is that no-one is going to stand up to

**4**

them. Look at the world we're living in, Paddy. Every country has lost a generation of men and far more besides. They're still rebuilding their homelands and their lives. It leaves countries like this vulnerable and unprotected."

"And that's where we come in."

"We can't be the world's police, though. It just doesn't work."

"As long as it works for Greta. We owe her."

Charles knew that he was right; they did owe her. A lot. She had provided so much intelligence, vital intel, her life on the line every day as she tried to get what was needed. He harboured no illusions. He knew exactly how she got her information. She was beautiful. She used that as a weapon, targeting some high-ranking officials, seducing them and interrogating them in pillow talk. He would never have said it aloud, though. That was the problem with being in love with someone.

They both loved her. That was another wrinkle to the rescue. Both men had fallen for her unique charms, and that meant they'd take too many risks to get her out, put each other in compromised situations if there was a chance it would help her. But that was something else that neither would admit. So they focused on getting her safe, knowing there would be fallout if they ever got back to Britain.

More gunfire outside.

More shouts.

Someone peeled away from the shadows and started running.

There had been no warning.

Charles watched in horror as a single shot punched into the man's back and he went down. There had been a moment, as the body fell to the ground, when his gut had clenched, sure that it wasn't a man at all, but a woman. Greta.

It wasn't.

But it could have been.

If she was out there, he willed her to stay put.

Hidden.

Neither of them spoke as they watched a soldier walk towards the fallen man, injured but still alive. The soldier drew a pistol from his holster and fired two more bullets that made the body dance on the ground before it was finally still.

The execution was more posturing, just like the tanks.

He doubted the soldiers would fire another shot in anger for a while, as long as no-one posed a threat. They'd laid down their marker. How long that would last was open to question. What was certain was that the Russians wouldn't waste time asking any.

"As long as they are out there, she's not going to be able to come in from the cold."

"We have to try to get a message to her."

Though how they could do that if she didn't want to be found was up for debate. There was a network of people down there, spread throughout the city, all carefully cultivated, loyalties bought and paid for, prepared to pass messages from one to another; people who could be trusted, people like Greta who put their lives at risk for the country they loved. And now that the Russians were no longer just on the doorstep, but very much inside the borders, the risks their resistance carried were so much greater. Could they still be trusted? Would they betray the British to new paymasters? What if a link in the chain broke? What if they were compromised? None of them knew more than the person who contacted them and the one they passed information on to, but if there was a break in the chain, there were links that could eventually lead back to them.

"Then one of us needs to go outside," Paddy said.

"It's going to be hard to move around in daylight." Charles looked out at the body lying in the street. A pool of dark blood had spread out around him.

"Problem is, it's now or never if we are going to make something happen. The alternative is we sit tight and wait. Is that what you want to do?"

"No," he admitted. Waiting would be unbearable.

# TWO

## February 1996

Sir Charles leaned back in his chair, sinking into the leather of the Chesterfield and savouring the taste of the cognac. It tasted every bit as expensive as it was. He appreciated the finer things in life.

A glance around revealed middle-aged and elderly men enjoying their own company: power brokers, prime movers, many enjoying an after-dinner cigar.

There was an amiable silence, punctuated by the occasional cough and the chink of ice against glass.

This was a haven from the hustle and bustle of London. Somewhere they could leave the worries of the world outside the ancient front door.

This had been his father's club, and his father's before him. His membership had been a formality. This luxurious leather armchair was akin to his inheritance.

He was skimming the headlines on the Evening Standard when a waiter appeared at his side. The man leaned down to speak to him.

"A visitor for you, sir," the man in the white jacket said, holding out a silver tray with a single white card on it.

Sir Charles picked it up. He read the name 'Michael Dawson'; a plain name, no doubt for a plain man. The absence of any kind of identification beyond a name and mobile telephone number that could have anyone at the other end was precisely how the Secret Service operated. He didn't need to have anything spelled out for him. After all, who else would come looking for him at this hour? He had been hoping for a quiet evening, but it would be rude to send the man away without at least speaking to him. If he were trouble, Sir Charles would simply have him ejected from the club.

He nodded to the waiter and indicated that the visitor should be shown in.

A moment later the man was ushered into the chair opposite him. As Michael Dawson sat down, the white-coated steward didn't make eye contact with him, but instead looked to Sir Charles for further instructions.

"Two more of these please, George," he said holding up the glass for the steward to take.

"No, no, it's fine," Dawson protested.

"Nonsense. You are my guest. Besides, it's rude to refuse my hospitality."

"Very good, sir," the steward said, then he disappeared into the background, like another wisp of smoke from all those expensive cigars.

"Thank you for seeing me, Sir Charles," Dawson said.

"I would say it is my pleasure, but I suspect it won't be." Sir Charles Wyndham pursed his lips. Truth be told, he was more than a little annoyed by the intrusion into his routine. He was a man who liked his rituals. "I get the distinct impression you're one of their terriers and that had I exercised my right of refusal, you would have simply hounded me until I relented, anyway. Better a civilised sit-down like this than to be

**9**

bundled into the back of a state car with tinted windows and driven away at high speed. Isn't that how Military Intelligence operates, nowadays?"

"Oh, I think you've been watching too much television, Sir Charles. We may be keen to talk to you, but we don't resort to kidnapping. That's not our style."

"At least not your own people?"

The man's expression did not change. He unzipped the document case he carried with him. Dawson pulled a photograph from the case and handed it over.

"Do you recognise this man?"

It was a still from a surveillance camera, but it had been blown up and manipulated to concentrate on one face caught looking up from a crowd of people.

Sir Charles hadn't seen the man for a very long time, and had thought he would never see him again. He was older now, but then they all were. Despite the years, there was no doubting who it was.

"Patrick O'Dwyer," he said. "Time has not been kind to either of us."

But then, they had both been through a lot since they had last seen each other. Times changed, people changed with them, or they perished. Sir Charles had decided that fieldwork wasn't for him and had resigned his commission to take over as the master at Nonesuch Manor following the death of his father. The new role hadn't come easily to him. After a few years he had found that he became more hands on in the day-to-day running of the estate than his father had ever been. Conversely, Paddy had dropped off the radar shortly after the events in Prague. The last he had heard, through channels, had been a red flag: suspicions raised that O'Dwyer had become involved with the IRA. There was something inevitable about it, despite his loyalties, or because of them. Paddy's ideologies aligned him with the struggle, but Sir Charles had never thought he would turn against Queen and country. But maybe that was what it was all about.

"He was caught on camera only three days ago," Dawson said.

"Where?" Sir Charles felt his heart rate increase, just a little, and tried not to look up too quickly. He didn't want to appear too eager. He was out of the game. They needed him: that much was obvious. But that didn't mean he had to roll over and beg. Why else would they have sought him out? He knew he wouldn't say no, but the very least he could do was make them work for it. No-one valued anything that came cheaply, especially not MI5.

"Fishguard."

"I'm surprised that the Welsh have CCTV," he offered. It was a good entry point for a wanted man; less conspicuous than if he had flown in to one of the major airports.

"We lost him within twenty minutes of him arriving."

"Of course you did." It wasn't an accusation, just a statement of fact. Paddy would have known there would be security in place, no matter how lax, even in an out-of-the-way ferry port like Fishguard. He would also know that maintaining surveillance would be next to impossible once he stepped outside the port into the town proper. He wasn't an idiot.

"He came over as a foot passenger. There's no evidence that he hired a car at the terminal."

"Was he travelling alone?"

"According to the manifest, he was."

"That doesn't mean very much. Is there footage from on the ferry? In his place, I would have made the journey on foot, my back-up in a car already on a different ferry before I ever set foot on it. He would have travelled over the day before, or even a few days earlier. Into a different port. It wouldn't be difficult to arrange a meet, to allow us to travel on together once we made landfall."

"I've got a list of all the passengers..." Dawson started fishing into his case again, but Sir Charles stopped him.

"That won't tell you anything. Certainly not if he's planning anything. You've got to proceed under the assumption his accomplice came over on a different ferry and that they are driving in a car with a UK number plate. No matter how many Irish cars come over on the ferry, they still stand out on the roads of this country. They won't rent, either. It's not expensive to pick up a reliable second-hand car. They have the funds. He, or maybe she, will have bought it privately, so it'll already be taxed and they won't have been asked for insurance documents. And, of course, they will have paid cash. The DVLA won't have been notified of the change of ownership yet and even if they have, a false name and address will have been given." It made sense. That was exactly how he would have done it, and given who had trained him and drilled into him how to think, that was exactly as Paddy O'Dwyer would have done it.

"You seem to know the man well."

"You know I do."

He returned the photograph to the intelligence officer, who slipped it back into his document case.

"And you know why. We trained together, we fought together." He resisted the temptation to say, We loved and lost the same woman. "I know what he would do because it's what I would do."

"That's what we were hoping you'd say."

"Just because I know and understand him doesn't mean that I'm prepared to get up close and personal with him. Once was enough. You should know that from the off. I know you think I'll be able to spot him, no matter what kind of disguise he might have adopted, but it goes both ways. He'd know me."

"I'm sorry," Dawson said. "I haven't made myself clear, have I? We have no interest in bringing you out of retirement only to risk you on the front line."

"Then what do you want?" Sir Charles asked.

"We want you to run a team of agents to stop him, and men like him. You're the best man for the job. There's no doubt about that. Control is adamant you are the only man who can provide the kind of insight we need."

"Flattery? I wouldn't have thought that was in the Service's arsenal. I'm sure that you have more than enough good people capable of dealing with this threat."

"Absolutely. We have good people more than capable of doing whatever it takes. What we are missing is someone who can put them in the right places at the right time."

"That's what intelligence is for."

"Intel provides the pieces of the puzzle, not the overview. You know that."

"And I suppose this means you have intelligence to suggest there is something major planned? Beyond the usual, I mean."

"We have unconfirmed reports of missing Semtex and, given the political convention season ahead of us, it would be remiss not to be on our guard. O'Dwyer's arrival is cause for concern."

Sir Charles thought about it for a moment. The man was right; it wasn't a coincidence. O'Dwyer was dangerous, even if he wasn't here to get his hands dirty. He'd changed sides. That made finding him a priority.

# THREE

## August 1968

 Charles waited in the alley, keeping himself tucked tight into the shadows.

They had drawn straws to decide who would go out. He'd lost. That said, there was no way he would have wanted Paddy to go out into the night while there were so many Russians in the streets. It wasn't that he was afraid that the Irishman would blow their cover, but Paddy's judgement was clouded. He couldn't trust him to make the hard call if he needed to. Love did that to a man. He was already a risk taker. If there were even the remotest chance of getting Greta out, he'd take it. And if the enemy knew that, then it would cost them. Charles knew that this was his chance to change things. They had one throw of the dice. One chance to get out of the city before they were discovered.

Charles carried his gun tucked into the top of his trousers at the back; he normally wore it in a shoulder holster, but this was expediency. It would be easier to dispose of the gun if he was captured than to ditch a leather holster. Unarmed, he could at least try to talk his way out of whatever trouble he got himself into. With a holster, even sans weapon, they'd shoot first, judging him an enemy combatant. The enemy didn't waste time asking questions. He could hardly raise his hands and claim the protections of the Geneva Convention. There would be no record of his death, no marker on his grave, no one to remember him. And that was preferable to the fate that waited for him if they had even an inkling he was a British agent. The gun was a better way out than being shipped to Moscow.

There were soldiers at street corners, huddled close together, not far from the burning braziers despite the fact the night air had barely lost any of the intense heat of the day. They hadn't crushed the barricades that had been erected by the locals opposed to the occupation. Yet. That was such a powerful word. It meant it was coming. Soon. It hadn't taken the invasion forces long to clear the roads and make it this far. The buildings bore the scars of gunfire pitting their façades, tears on the face of the city. There was precious little anyone could do to halt the red tide now the tanks were rolling. Even the burnt out cars were no real hindrance. The tanks could push them to one side or roll straight over them if they chose, but right now it seemed to Charles that they had little interest in engaging. That would change. The more the locals fought back, the more desperate they became, the tighter the occupier's fist would clench around them, choking the life out of Prague.

There was a dead letter drop a few streets from the house. He was banking on there being news waiting for him. He carried a note to drop off to ensure their current situation was relayed to Control: second best, but preferable to their own position being given away if they risked their own radio. Whoever unloaded the dead drop would take the message to a relay station outside the city. Somewhere remote. Shifting the risk from them.

Heavy boots crunched broken glass underfoot.

Two soldiers walked past the alley where he hid.

Charles didn't breathe.

Didn't move.

He timed them, silently counting down how long it took the pair to complete a circuit of the streets they patrolled. Four minutes. But that left less than one minute when this section was out of sight, meaning he had barely enough time to make his way out of the alley's mouth and across the road to find another hiding place before they passed once more.

It was going to be a painstaking journey through the streets.

He couldn't allow his vigilance to drop for a moment, even when he reached the other side of the barricades.

Even there, on the 'safe' side of the street, he knew all too well that there would be traitors ready to sell out the foreigner to the Russians in return for favours or reward. It was the same the world over. Wars changed, uniforms changed, sides changed, people didn't.

He moved silently, careful not to kick or scuff his feet against any debris lying in the alleyway; the last thing he wanted was to draw attention to his presence, even if they were arrogant enough to believe that only cats and dogs were stupid enough to break the curfew that kept the city near-silent.

Charles listened for the sound of boots in the street, counting the rhythm of their steps as they approached his new position.

He pressed against the wall, feeling the cold brick at his back, trying to shrink as deeply into the darkness as he could—becoming part of it.

On this circuit the soldiers took closer interest in the gaps between houses, the rubble strewn in front and any darker place where someone could be hiding. Not good. Had something happened to make them more suspicious? A rocket up the arse by their commanding officer for not taking the task seriously enough, maybe? Charles wasn't going to take any risks. But he couldn't stay there forever. Standing still was as big a gamble as moving now. The only way was forward.

Eventually, the sound of the footsteps began to recede.

He chanced moving a little closer to the edge of the building, trying to catch a glimpse of their location, pulling back quickly again when he spotted a second pair of soldiers coming around the corner.

One of them shouted something.

He'd been seen.

"Shit!" Charles hissed under his breath.

Where the hell had they come from?

He doubled back along the alley, hoping that the other streets would be empty. He couldn't head back to the safe house. He needed to lead them a merry dance through the city first. There was the old Jewish cemetery not too far away, and the warren of streets around there that might work, doubling back towards the train station. Ideally, he would have crossed the *Karlův most,* the Charles Bridge, into another part of the city altogether, disappearing around the castle or down by the riverside, but he had no idea what streets were under surveillance. He couldn't risk being caught here, though. Not this close to the safe house. If they started kicking in doors it would only be a matter of time before they stumbled on Paddy. At best, they would be an embarrassment to the British government and a pair of pawns in negotiations that led to a few Russians being traded. He didn't want to think what the worst case might be. It wouldn't help him.

At last he thought the road was clear and made a break for it, head down, arms and legs pumping furiously, teeth gritted against the icy cold, sprinting from one side of the street to the other.

The silence was broken by another shout in Russian followed by a word that he at least understood: "Zastavit!" Stop.

But he couldn't stop; he had to keep running as if his very life depended on it, because it did.

He was barely into his stride when the first shot rang out.

He made it to the other side, breathing hard, and dipped into another alleyway, stumbling across a pile of debris that had been abandoned there. He slipped, tried to steady himself against the wall, kept himself upright and scrambled over the obstacle.

Blindly running into the darkness, he slammed into a closed door at the far end of the alleyway.

A dead end.

He cursed himself.

No way out.

No way back.

His only hope was that the soldier hadn't seen which of the alleys he had ducked into. And even then, that only offered a few extra minutes, at best. It wouldn't take them long to run him down.

He'd made the mistake that was going to get him killed.

He pressed himself against the wall and waited.

There was nothing else he could do.

He stared out at the street, hoping that he'd catch sight of the silhouette of the soldier passing by. Then maybe he could step out behind him, break his neck and be gone before anyone could call for help.

There was no thunder of boots on the street.

No reinforcements.

Charles waited, fist clenching and unclenching, mouth dry, heart hammering against his breastbone. Everything seemed so much more vivid. More real.

At last the shadow appeared at the opening of the narrow passageway.

He held his breath.

# FOUR

## February 1996

Sir Charles slept fitfully that night, his mind turning the events of the past over and over. Images that he thought he'd finally managed to escape haunted him every bit as effectively as Jacob Marley's chains.

He had been through enough in his life—more than enough—and had been naïve to believe he'd finally left it all behind. It had only taken a single photograph to shatter his illusions. It wasn't so much the sight of Patrick O'Dwyer that had put his thoughts into turmoil; it was the other memories it triggered. Memories of Greta, the woman he had abandoned, and what doing that had cost him.

Eventually he gave up on the search for sleep and turned on the small bedside light. If the images wouldn't go away, he would just have to face them. The dossier may have been about O'Dwyer, but there was a chance that he might learn about what had become of her. What he would have done to read a single paragraph describing how Greta was alive and well and living with a family of her own. That would have been the win scenario. Part of him would be just as relieved to discover she had been dead even before they had made their escape. He was looking for a way to salve his conscience, but he knew that the truth was going to be painful. He didn't want to know that by walking away, he'd delivered her into the wrong hands, even if that was the truth. They would have made her spill her guts, even if she had little knowledge of any real worth. The people she knew, half a dozen contacts, were long gone. She might have been part of brokering their freedom. But that wouldn't have stopped the Russians breaking her, thinking she knew more and determined to find out what, even if it killed her. The Greta he'd known would have held out for as long as she could, but everyone has a breaking point.

The file was considerably slimmer than his own, which he'd caught sight of when being sounded out for a job more than twenty years ago. Even then, it looked like the green treasury tags, which held the pages in place inside the battered card file, were straining to contain all of his crimes and misdemeanours in the eyes of Her Majesty, along with a record of the things he'd got right.

He wondered just how thick that file might be now.

He started from the back of the file: the earliest documents giving details of his recruitment and career. There had been concerns from the beginning over his Irish Republican sympathies, but there was no denying that Patrick O'Dwyer had skills that were much in demand at the time, and, far from being a hindrance, his accent set him apart from the public school and university-educated young men brought into the Service purely for their intelligence and that supercilious air of superiority they'd mastered at Oxbridge. Even back then, Charles had known that he belonged to that group, the privileged few, silver spoon and all, destined for greatness in their own right without having to break a sweat.

At least things had changed since those bad old, sad old days. Not enough, though. Privilege was still privilege if your face fitted.

Unsurprisingly, he had been watched every bit as much as he had been a watcher. Sir Charles hadn't realised it at the time. He had never been asked to provide reports on his activities when they had been in the field together, so he could only assume that Control had feared any such tittle-tattle would have compromised their ability to work together, to trust each other. Better he not question the Irishman's loyalty. There had been a time, though, when he had realised that he was the only one he could rely on, that Control was prepared to hang him out to dry if the worst came to the worst.

Sir Charles' hand trembled slightly when he got close to the pages that would hold the record of their time together in Prague, knowing that this was where he risked finding out the truth about Greta. Once he turned the page, he'd no longer be able to imagine her out there, living brilliantly. He'd know.

Or wouldn't.

The page had been redacted. The file contained a note to say that pages concerning certain events had been removed. There was a reference number, which meant nothing to him. Maybe it was pure coincidence that those particular pages were the ones that had been removed before the file reached him. Maybe it wasn't.

Sir Charles followed the reports that covered the Irishman's service after the two of them had gone their separate ways.

He'd heard of nothing unusual about any of O'Dwyer's missions until the day he had announced that he'd had enough and was quitting. O'Dwyer disappeared without returning to be debriefed. The sounds of panic had echoed through the quiet backrooms of Whitehall as codes and passwords were changed in a flurry of panicked activity, chains of contact and command altered to keep field operatives from being exposed, word going out to be hyper-alert in case they'd been compromised.

Fear was king in those days.

If O'Dwyer defected then every agent he'd ever come into contact with was compromised.

Sir Charles had never shared that fear.

It wasn't in O'Dwyer's make-up to take the enemy's hand and do that particular dance with the devil.

That he was out meant he'd drawn a line under this part of his life, and had other priorities now. Wounds take time to heal. Wounds like Greta might never scab over.

Something was wrong, though.

He scanned page after page of reports, most of them covering incidents that he was aware of, coming across snippets of information that concerned him rather than O'Dwyer, tiny things that he hadn't been aware of at the time. Once he'd left the service there were a number of detailed surveillance reports, pages filled with the lives of known associates, some of them with cross-reference numbers which indicated that they had files of their own. Most of the names meant nothing to him, but a couple of them, he was sure, had been involved with one of the bombings on the mainland in the 1970s. Another was a prominent figure in Sinn Fein. They had begun to gain a certain amount of legitimacy, but there was a long way to go before they would be considered more than merely the political wing of the IRA.

He didn't know why he was so surprised to discover that O'Dwyer was married and that he had two sons. So many people he had known within the Service had been unable to maintain a long-term relationship, never mind have a family.

Perhaps that was the reason why he had left: to find another path in the world? There were times when he'd thought there might even be a woman out there that he could love and who could love him. It hadn't happened, though. And wouldn't happen now.

He spent the next hour working his way through the facts, skipping over routine reports that had little to say, concentrating on those which implied that his old partner was involved with IRA activities. As he worked through the pages, the gaps between reports seemed to increase; missing time, which made no sense at all unless someone had decided that he no longer posed a risk. But if that had been the case, then there would have been a note to that effect. If he'd simply slipped beneath the radar, someone should have recorded that, too. If this was all the intelligence that was held on the man, then the only conclusion he could draw with any certainty was that someone, somewhere hadn't been doing his or her job.

The final report was dated two days ago and gave details of him having been identified from footage in Fishguard.

So now Paddy O'Dwyer was back in the country and had already given everyone the slip. Something didn't stack up. It felt wrong. Very wrong. Even as he read back through the notes, the omissions and routine reports, he was convinced that someone was being played. He couldn't help but think it was he.

Had O'Dwyer managed to control what information he allowed them to gather? Or were the people who were trying to enlist Sir Charles' help keeping things from him?

The problem was, the whole business was always about lies and omissions.

# FIVE

The shadow waited at the far end of the alley.

Charles held his breath, willing the figure to move on, to check the next passageway instead of entering the dead end he'd cornered himself in.

*Move. Go. Move on. Don't come this way*, and every variant of the thought crossed his mind.

One more step and he wouldn't have a choice, he'd have to take him out. If he were fast enough, maybe – just maybe – he'd be able to charge him down before he had the chance to bring his rifle to bear in such an enclosed space. It wasn't much, but surprise was the only weapon he had.

"*For Christ's sake, Charley*," the figure at the far end hissed. "*Get your arse out of there sharpish or we're both fucked.*"

"Paddy!" Charles struggled not to call his name at much more than a whisper. *Why the hell had he come out after him? Why had he put himself at risk? Had he seen something in the street that Charles hadn't?* The questions tumbled through his mind and stopped his brain from sending the messages it needed to, to make his legs move.

He had to get out of there fast.

He climbed back over the debris to join his partner, well aware that without his timely intervention he'd have been lying in a pool of his own blood in this dirty back alley.

"Thanks," he said. It was shorthand for 'I owe you my life'. They both knew it. That meant they didn't have to linger on it. He drew his Browning, his hand closing comfortably around the grip like old friends too long apart. The questions would have to wait until later: as long as there was a later.

"It won't be long before they realise one of their men is down, and when that happens, all hell is going to break loose. No going back, Charley. If we're going to get out of this alive we need to run, and keep running. And if we're lucky they'll find the safe house before they find Greta and the others. Even under torture, they can't give up what they don't know." It was cold, but that didn't make it any less true.

There were enough people in these streets: innocent people, still struggling to recover from the last time their country had been occupied. Protecting them wasn't a priority, though. Looking out for their own was. The last thing he wanted was for one of their informers to be caught up in a witch-hunt. There was enough in those rooms to identify the two of them as spies without shining a light on anyone else. At least he hoped so. But they had no way of getting a message back to Control now. They had to assume they were burned. London would carry on broadcasting, but without the key, the incoming messages would mean nothing. And without the appropriate responses, Control would know they were gone and cease transmission. That was protocol. What mattered now was getting themselves out of harm's way.

So they ran.

The only other person on the night-shrouded street was the body lying a hundred yards away.

No matter how much training they did, it could never be enough to prepare someone to run for their life.

Hitting the streets too hard, too fast, would only mean you burned through your reserves too quickly and you'd be on your knees long before the people you were running from. It was about pace—keeping it even. Too fast meant too much noise, as well. And no matter how quickly they ran, they couldn't outrun a bullet.

They needed to be smart.

He resisted the urge to look back. Looking back helped no-one.

As long as he didn't hear a challenge, he was going to keep on moving.

If they could just get around the corner, out of sight of any newcomers, they'd have a chance of getting away. There were places on the outskirts of the city where they would be able to hole up until extraction could be arranged, assuming they could get a message back to Control—which was a big ask when they couldn't trust anyone.

They turned the corner.

This time Charles looked back. He couldn't help himself.

The body was still there, alone, and that gave him hope. Hope was the worst. But maybe, just maybe, they would be able to slip away before the noose closed around their necks?

They maintained an easy rhythm together, running side-by-side.

Charles was a runner. He had good stamina. He liked hitting the track and stretching his legs. This was different. Different, even, from running with a full pack on his back for hours on end. Fear was more exhausting than distance travelled. He had no idea of how fit O'Dwyer was, given that he was a chain smoker and heavy drinker—a proper Irishman, he liked to call himself—but they were in this together. O'Dwyer'd saved his life back there. He'd carry the Irishman on his back if he had to.

The streets were different at night: another world.

It was impossible to tell which buildings had fallen to neglect, which had been ravaged in that previous conflict, and which bore the fresh wounds of the occupation. In daylight, it was clear that it would take a lot longer than the twenty years that had passed to erase every trace of damage in the city and rebuild, but at night they took on a timeless, haunted quality that made the damage so much harder to grasp.

He knew exactly why his mind was fixated on the old buildings. It kept the fear at bay and gave him something, other than the pain in his muscles, to think about. He covered distance without noticing. The shapes of buildings merged into one another as O'Dwyer led them through street after street, turning first one way, then another. They were moving away from the Russian-controlled streets into safe territory, but that wouldn't stop the enemy from following. It only meant they were less likely to run into a routine patrol. It also meant they were moving further and further away from the streets he was familiar with.

"This way," O'Dwyer rasped as Charles failed to see that he had turned off the side street into an even smaller passage between two crumbling buildings.

He paused and then turned after him, ducking under a sheet of corrugated iron that the Irishman pushed aside.

He waited as O'Dwyer stooped in behind him and replaced the barrier, then pressed against the wall to let the other man ease past him to lead the way. He pulled a torch from his jacket and turned the beam into another alleyway.

Something moved in the debris, paused, squeaked and scrabbled away.

"I fucking hate rats," said O'Dwyer, kicking at a piece of wood before taking another step.

They didn't see another as they made their way cautiously over the piles of rubble and stinking refuse. It was a city. There were millions of the things living under their feet, crawling through the ancient sewers. There would be dozens no more than a few yards away. Just because he couldn't see them didn't mean they weren't there. In conditions like this, people suffered while the rats thrived. Towards the end of the covered alley, O'Dwyer stopped at a green door set low in the wall. It came up no higher than his waist. He crouched down and gave four knocks: two fast, two slow. After a moment, Charles heard movement on the other side, followed by the sound of metal grating against metal and then the wooden door being scraped inward to reveal darkness. O'Dwyer shone his torch inside, revealing a man retreating down a short flight of wooden stairs. The door swung freely in the air.

"Quick," said O'Dwyer. "Inside. Mind your head."

Feeling like Alice, facing a door far too small for him to get through, Charles hunkered down and climbed backwards into the darkness. The torchlight dazzled him every time he looked up. He did his best to keep his head down, focused on where he was placing his feet until he felt an earth floor beneath him. A firm hand led him away from the wooden stair as O'Dwyer followed him down.

They weren't alone. An emaciated Slavic fellow stood with his back to them. He wore the white shirt of a waiter. He turned as O'Dwyer's partner pushed the door closed behind him, and drove the two bolts into place to secure it. Charles noted the deep shadows that accentuated the harsh bone structure. There was nothing forgiving about the man's face; nothing comforting. But that was good. He wasn't here looking for comfort.

"Charley, this is Hans. Hans, this is Charley. Hans, we need you to get a message back to Control for us." The other man nodded. "Charley, we'll be safe here until something is arranged."

"What is this place?"

"A safe house. Well, a safe cellar, if you want to be pedantic."

"Why didn't I know about this place?"

"For the same reason I don't know about yours," he replied, and Charles knew what he meant. He had a place, too. Somewhere he could have gone if his partner had been captured. A bolthole that couldn't be betrayed under interrogation. Two people couldn't keep a secret. It was the only way to guarantee you weren't betrayed. Of course they'd both been allocated places.

"How long before you'll be able to contact Control?" he asked Hans.

"Three hours," the other man said, tapping on his watch. "Three hours after midnight." He spoke in heavily accented English, clearly not his first language, maybe not even his second.

There were two mattresses on the floor, a table with two chairs and very little else other than a second flight of stairs that led up to a door, which no doubt led out of Wonderland and into the rest of the house.

Now that O'Dwyer had turned off his torch, the only light in the room came from an oil lamp on the table, which served to show how Spartan the space was. Charles wondered how much time Hans spent down in this place every day. Did he sleep here himself, just in case he was needed? Was that why there were two mattresses? Or, he reasoned, thinking properly for the first time that night, did he also offer a safe haven to another operative, someone else working in the city that they didn't even know existed?

# SIX

## February 1996

The car was waiting for him at nine.

Dawson, the official who had brought the file for him the previous evening, had wanted to send it for him earlier, but Sir Charles refused to be hurried from pillar to post.

He knew he was in danger of sliding gracelessly out of middle age and turning into a grumpy old man before his time, but whenever anyone tried to push him faster than he was prepared to move, or force him to give an answer he wasn't prepared to give, the answer was invariably 'no'. Dawson had come close to learning that the hard way.

The file on O'Dwyer was tucked safely in his briefcase. It hadn't left his side from the moment he'd been given it, including sitting on the table beside him as he had a breakfast of scrambled eggs and smoked salmon. Reading anything other than the morning's newspaper was an eyebrow-raising offense as far as most of the members were concerned, but he ignored their disapproving glances as he scanned through the pages yet again, determined to be sure that he hadn't missed a single thing; that there was no vital piece of information he was missing. By the time he slipped into the rear of the

Lexus, he was confident that he was as prepared as he could be. Aside from those few redacted pages and missing cross-references, he'd done everything humanly possible to make sure no-one could ambush him.

Dawson was waiting for him when the car pulled to a halt outside a plain building. There was no obvious indication of what lay inside, certainly nothing to say they were entering the corridors of power, but Sir Charles had been in places like this before. If a meeting was held off-site from the main seats of power, then any action was going to be treated as unofficial.

Unsanctioned.

In other words, deniable.

The conversation was going to be more than just a quiet request for help, that much was obvious.

The right people, the ones who rarely left the seclusion of their ivory towers, would know exactly what was about to transpire; but knowing and being responsible were very different beasts in the world of espionage. As long as any op wasn't sanctioned under their noses, as long as official papers weren't presented for them to sign, they could deny all knowledge, and that was good enough for them.

But Sir Charles was done with the cloak and dagger of this shadowy world.

He was prepared to give them a little of his time, the chance to question him about O'Dwyer. He owed them that much, but beyond that, nothing.

"Sir Charles," Dawson said, striding towards him with one hand outstretched. "Everything is ready for you. I trust you found the information of interest."

"It was a touch dry," he replied, noticing the fleeting look of disappointment the other man tried to hide. "But that was because you only let me see what you wanted me to see. I know the game."

"I'm sorry, I don't know what you mean." He was lying. He wasn't good at it, either. Sir Charles' entire life had been based around lies and recognising when someone was lying to him; he would have known if Dawson was being duped too, but that feigned innocence was one that screamed 'Found out'. It probably wasn't the young man's idea, but he certainly knew what had been done to the file. That was a mistake. Better to be kept in the dark so he couldn't be caught out in a lie. The old man was just better at this game.

"Well, let's have a chat with your lords and masters, shall we? I'm interested to hear what they have to say about things. I should probably warn you before you fasten your flag to their mast: they're seldom as clever as they think they are."

Dawson chuckled at that.

He didn't disagree.

Before being shown down the hallway, a heavily-built man who would have looked a lot more comfortable in camouflage fatigues invited him to empty his pockets into a plastic tray and ran a scanner over his body and case. The man did his work in silence.

Sir Charles had met his type plenty of times. It was in the eyes. He was the kind of man that could kill without compunction, without questioning orders. He was nothing like Dawson, whose skill he suspected lay in data and in detail, not in death.

The man gave a nod to Dawson once his check was complete, but remained silent and unsmiling, and in the way.

"This way, please, Sir Charles," said Dawson, beckoning him to follow him around the man mountain. "Just a formality, you understand. But we can't afford to take any chances."

Of course he understood.

He had been part of this world for longer than he had wanted and would have been disturbed if he'd been waved through without protocol being followed to the letter.

Dawson stopped when he reached a nondescript door off the passage.

He took a moment to straighten his tie while Sir Charles tried not to smile at the habitual action, then knocked three times: not too timid, not too aggressive. It was a well-practised knock intended to make a statement about him. It was the kind of thing that paper-pushers took pride in, but Sir Charles had more respect for the man by the front door that had been thorough in his search, and for the driver who had picked him up from his club. They were cogs in the machine that knew their role and did it to the best of their ability without worrying about what anyone else might think of them.

"Come in," called a voice from inside.

Dawson opened the door and stepped aside for Sir Charles to go in.

He didn't follow him in.

He closed the door behind him.

The room was bare of any kind of decoration or ornamentation, as so many of these kinds of places tended to be. This was no-one's office, but neither was it an interrogation room. He had been debriefed in rooms like this, where the whole point of the whiteness was to offer nothing for the imagination to feed off. The debriefs were rigorous, the same questions coming over and over again to test his story, make sure that it stood up and that he'd given everything he could give. Those sessions had never been pleasant, but they were necessary, and everyone was on the same side.

This time, though, he got the distinct impression that wasn't quite the case.

Two men sat on one side of the simple table, leaving another chair free on the opposite side. "Not expecting company, then?" Sir Charles said as he took his place without waiting to be asked. He fixed his stare on the two men: one, then the other, while they returned his gaze.

"Thank you for coming," one of them said at last.

He raised an eyebrow at that, deliberately theatrical. "I had a choice?"

"Of course you did. We are asking for your help. We're not holding you hostage."

"Indeed? Then why are you hiding things from me?"

"I don't understand."

Sir Charles inclined his head slightly, breathed in, nostrils flaring. "I'm going to give you one chance, only one. Don't talk to me as if I'm still wet behind the ears." He reached inside his briefcase and pulled the file out, and threw it down onto the table between them. It skidded along its surface. "Why only give me half of the file?"

"We gave you everything we have on this man," the man lied. He was better at it than Dawson, but still not good. He knew he no longer had the upper hand, but still he insisted that the file was complete.

"Then we are done here, gentleman," said Sir Charles closing his briefcase and getting back to his feet. "Maybe another time."

"Wait," the silent man said. "Please. Sit down for a moment."

Sir Charles already had his back to them and allowed himself the smallest of smiles before turning back to face them. "I said one chance. You wasted it." He was sure, now, just how badly they needed him. He could demand whatever price he wanted. He didn't sit, but neither did he leave. He stood behind his chair, expression blank, and waited to hear what they had to say.

"You are correct. There is certain information that was removed, sensitive information that relates to agents that are still active. I did not wish to compromise their current situation."

"Which translates to: you don't trust me."

"Don't take it personally, old boy. I don't trust *anyone*."

"Good answer," said Sir Charles. "But if you don't trust me, what do you want from me?"

"Your old friend O'Dwyer..."

"Let's get one thing straight: he was never my friend. We were colleagues, comrades in arms. I trusted him with my life, but we were not friends."

"I assume because you were also rivals in love," the man said.

Sir Charles felt a sudden dryness in his mouth, but tried not to show it. They were right and they knew it. Which meant they'd done their research. But how could they know? He'd never told a soul. It was a secret he'd intended to take to the grave. What else did they know about Prague? Greta. He could hardly bear to think her name still, even after all this time, let alone say it out loud.

"You asked too many question after you came back," the man said, answering his question without him needing to ask it. "It's not unusual for someone to return filled with worry for someone left behind; all you need to do is study their body language. It's amazing what we communicate without realizing, especially when we're worrying about someone we've become involved with."

He paused for a moment, offering Sir Charles the opportunity to deny it. He knew what the rules were, he always had, but sometimes there were things that were hard to fight. Being with O'Dwyer back then, holed up in a city under siege, had not been the easiest of times.

"O'Dwyer was the same."

"What happened to her?" Sir Charles asked. "What happened to the girl? Tell me that, and we can talk."

The man shrugged, clearly thinking that it was no concern of his. "I don't know. I might be able to find out," he said. "But it won't be easy."

And now he understood. They were playing him. They'd hooked him with the file, knowing that would be enough to get him to meet face-to-face. They were offering answers in return for getting back into bed with them. The question was: how badly did he need to know those answers?

Until yesterday he'd been quite content to imagine her making a new life for herself even though he wasn't part of it. Then they'd turned up at his door and brought reality with them. He didn't have to imagine. He could find out the truth. But did he want that? Really? Deep down? Who would it help to know that she'd been beaten, tortured and then executed by the Russians twenty years ago?

"What do you want me to do?"

The man nodded, the bargain struck. There would be no going back. "You already know that O'Dwyer is in the country."

"I've read the file."

"We believe we know why he is here."

"Of course you do. You knew yesterday when you sent Dawson to bring me in." Mind games.

"We think he's here to build a bomb."

"Alright." He did his best to keep any of the groundswell of anger at the betrayal he felt out of his voice and asked, "What do you think that I can do that your own men can't?"

"You know him of old. You can think like he does. You know the kind of places he might eat, where he might drink; even on the most basic levels, you know how he talks, you know how he walks. You're the one person we have who really knows Patrick O'Dwyer. We don't have anyone who's been as close to him as you have. We want you to help find him. He needs to be stopped."

# SEVEN

For three days, they remained inside the cellar; three days without sunlight or fresh air.

Hans came and went with food and water, nothing extravagant or particularly tasty, but after three days in the hole it could have been ambrosia. He emptied the bucket they used as a toilet. It was not exactly hell down there, but it was a long way from comfortable. At night they lay awake until exhaustion claimed them, listening to the scratch of the rats in the walls.

On the third day they rose from their tomb.

It was not a spiritual occurrence.

"Come, now," Hans said, clambering up the wooden steps. He unbolted the door to let them out. "End of next street you see a lorry. It wait for you. Hide in back. Quick. Quick. Go."

Charles did not need to be told twice.

He clambered up the wooden stairs first, O'Dwyer adding his thanks to the few words Charles had uttered, and then they were out in the air for the first time in what felt like forever. The alley was in darkness just as it had been when they'd arrived, but at the far end there was a faint glow of light, sunrise only moments away. They skirted close to the building, even though there was no-one in the street, moving quickly. His legs felt like rubber after three days of sitting around. As promised, the lorry was a couple of hundred yards away, but it seemed so much further. They walked as silently as they could, resisting the urge to break into a run.

The back of the lorry was covered with tarpaulin that hid a variety of pieces of furniture; someone was moving out of the city. Charles slid underneath, squeezing beneath a table to give O'Dwyer space to follow him in.

He assumed the driver knew what he was transporting. A few minutes later, he heard the crunch of boots and the lash of ropes being secured, pinning the covering in place. Children laughed and scrambled into the cab followed by the unmistakable sound of their mother's voice gently scolding them. Charles could not make out a single word, just the rise and fall of her voice. A moment later, the engine started, sending a vibration through the flatbed and every item of furniture in the back; then they were moving.

Twice the lorry stopped and the driver spoke.

Again, the voices were muffled. Both male, this time. Soldiers, he assumed, though no-one bothered to check the load for stowaways. Perhaps it was just routine, or maybe the gaggle of small children had distracted the search party. He didn't care, because a few minutes later they were out of the city and jouncing and juddering along the rutted road towards safety.

"So you're telling me you weren't tipped off about my bolt-hole? No-one offered it as a backup in case yours was compromised?" O'Dwyer tried to make conversation in the dark as they bounced along.

"I've already told you, Paddy, I hadn't even thought about it."

"But you must have *known*. Surely?"

"What can I say? Too much on my mind without worrying it."

41

"Well, I'm telling you this for nothing: if they saddled the Irishman with a shithole and gave you a palace, I'm putting in a complaint," O'Dwyer said.

"Attic room above a shop."

"Groceries on tap then?"

"Puncture repair kits," he said. "It was a bicycle repair shop."

"Could have been worse. You might have had rats for neighbours."

"True. You win." The old couple that owned the shop had done the same more than twenty years before, helping hide people from the Nazis. They'd lived long enough to see that what had taken their place wasn't so much better, only different.

The lorry came to another juddering halt.

This time the engine was turned off.

The vehicle continued to rumble and shudder for a moment, and then they heard the lash of ropes slithering back against the tarpaulin. Charles reached for his gun. When the sun came streaming into their hidey-hole, there was no guarantee they'd see a smiling face. He heard the kids' laughter and relaxed a little.

"Time to go," their father said as he peeled the tarpaulin back.

Charles blinked at the blinding sunlight.

They clambered out of the back, trying not to upset the delicate balance that held the furniture in place.

"Thank you," said Charles as two small girls appeared around the side of the truck, emphasising just how much the man had risked to get them out. "Where are we?"

"Safe," he said. "That's all that matters. Follow this track," he gestured off to the right. "There is a footbridge at the bottom, maybe a mile. Someone will be waiting for you."

Charles wanted to give him more than just thanks, but he had nothing that would be of any value to them. He needed his gun and his pockets were empty save for a couple of coins. Money would seem like an insult, he was sure, but he took a couple of coins out anyway and gave one each to the children, telling them not to spend it all at once. The man smiled at the gesture and ushered the children back inside the cab. He secured the ropes again then climbed back behind the wheel. A couple of seconds later the engine roared back to life and with the sound of grating gears, the lorry pulled away.

They set off down the dirt track, cold, tired, but alive.

That was all they could have hoped for.

*   *   *

It was another three days before they reached England.

They passed through the hands of several couriers, sleeping in safe houses with the mood lightening with each passing mile. New papers were provided to get them through one border crossing after another until the white cliffs of Dover were in sight. But Charles knew that this wouldn't be the end of it. It couldn't be. There would be the endless debrief as information was collected and collated, checked and doubled checked, until Control was happy that the report to be placed on file was complete and accurate.

And then there would be the guilt that came with leaving someone behind.

That would never go away.

# EIGHT

## February 1996

Sir Charles was glad to get out of the room, out of the building. He felt dirty.

There was a reason he'd turned his back on people like that. They were snakes. Oleaginous.

The car waited to take him wherever he wanted to go. His driver had been replaced by the soldier who'd scanned him through security on the way into the building.

"The name's Terry, Sir Charles. I'll be at your disposal for as long as you need me."

"How involved are you in what's going on, soldier?"

"Not very. I know you're the key to stopping a man who needs to be stopped. That's it."

"That's one way of putting it."

"I was being polite, sir. My first instinct was to say: there's a piece of shit out there intent on causing mischief, and we need to make sure the only thing left of him's the skid marks, if you'll pardon my French."

Sir Charles couldn't stop himself from laughing. The man was a breath of fresh air after being cooped up with the starched shirts whose greatest fear was a paper cut. Terry was a front line soldier. He knew what it was like be in fear of his life, going toe-to-toe with the PLF and IRA and other enemies of the state. He had that air about him. He was a survivor. "I think you and I will get on just fine, " he said.

"Thank you, sir."

"Where have you served, soldier?" It wasn't a question of 'if'; it was only 'where'.

"A couple of tours of Northern Ireland. The Falklands."

"Not easy places."

"No, sir. Not easy at all."

"Sounds like you're the perfect man for the job."

"Glad to hear it, sir. Where to?"

"There's an Irish bar near the Elephant and Castle called The Shamrock, do you know it?"

"Indeed I do, sir, though it's changed its name. It's called Malone's, now. Not the classiest of places, if you know what I mean."

"I'm not after class."

"The new owner invested in a pot of paint and put the prices up, but the clientele is the same."

"Which is exactly what I was hoping to hear. I'm rather hoping to bump into someone who used to be a fixture in the old place."

"Will you want me to come in with you, sir?"

"Best if you wait outside. Don't want to scare him off. These people have a knack of sniffing out the enemy. I'd rather get thrown out than have chairs thrown, if you catch my meaning." It wasn't subtle. Sir Charles was an old man, Terry, on the other hand, was a brute more than capable of taking care of himself. His presence inside a notorious Republican boozer would only serve to antagonise the Irish boys, turning a tricky situation into a brawl.

"If you're sure, sir. I'll be right outside the door. All you have to do is yell."

"Thank you, Terry."

They drove through heavy traffic. Sir Charles always found the urban crawl frustrating. He had no patience for the city. Driving in London was like being stuck somewhere around Dante's fourth circle.

Given the choice, he would have avoided the capital altogether and remained in the family home, concentrating on the renovations to the house. Nonesuch Manor had been in his family for generations, but, barring a miracle, he would be the last Wyndham to occupy it. That didn't mean that he couldn't make the most of the place for as long as he was able. The only problem was going to be raising the kind of money necessary to do what was needed, let alone what he wanted to do. Yes, he could gouge Her Majesty for plenty of cash to finance the op. All he had to do was track down O'Dwyer. But it felt like selling his soul.

The obvious starting place was Jimmy Shannon. Assuming, that was, that he was still alive. The last time Sir Charles had seen him, Jimmy had been on a three-week bender that showed no sign of stopping. The boy seemed intent on drinking the bar dry singlehandedly. Before that, he had been on the fringes of the Republican movement, but something had changed him, causing him to tie his colours to the mast. He'd become a hero to some, a terrorist to others.

But that had been a long time ago.

Even if he was still alive, there was no guarantee he'd talk.

Still, Sir Charles had to start somewhere, and that somewhere was the snug of a bar in the Elephant and Castle.

Jimmy was in the same seat he'd been in almost a decade earlier. It was as if the pub had been repainted around him.

"Jimmy," Sir Charles said, placing a double measure of Bushmills in front of him.

The man looked up with whiskey-sodden eyes that had trouble focusing.

It took him a moment to place the voice because the years had changed the face. Then recognition managed to work its way across his brain.

"Charley!" the man slurred, starting to get to his feet before thinking better of it and slumping back down again. "I thought you were dead. You're not dead, are you?"

"I'm not dead," Sir Charles said. "I thought you might be, though. It's good to see you're not." He took a seat opposite the Irishman. The pub was quiet enough that the few people in the bar had turned to take a look at him as walked in, and listened as he ordered drinks before going to join Jimmy. But now he was sitting down they ignored him. All but one: a young man who had slipped out though through the door marked 'Toilets'. He was too young to have been a regular the last time he'd been in the bar. He was either making a call or flushing away something that shouldn't have been in his pockets. The latter, most likely. If he'd been older, Sir Charles would have been more concerned, but it was very unlikely the kid knew who he was.

"Oh no, I'm not going anywhere in a hurry, Charley. I'll be here until they pull this old shitter down around my head."

Sir Charles caught the barman's eye roll. Obviously he suspected the same thing. He waited until the man's attention was drawn to another drinker who wanted a refill before he gave Jimmy his full attention.

"Have you seen anything of Paddy lately?"

"I've seen a lot of Paddies. A lot of Micks too. Common name. Every fucker's a Paddy. You looking for any particular

**47**

Paddy?" Then Jimmy realised who he meant. Sir Charles had only ever been to the pub with one Paddy, and had never spoken to Jimmy without him being there. His expression changed as if he'd suddenly sobered up.

"I don't know anything about him. Haven't heard a thing about him in years. Last I heard he was in France. Or maybe it was Spain. Somewhere warm, and away from here. Nasty fucker."

"We both know that's not true, don't we, Jimmy? Even I know that last week he was in Omagh. Thing is, he's not there now."

"Sure he is. He'll be lying drunk under a table in a bar somewhere, counting out his sorrows. That's where you should be looking for him. Search the pubs in the whole of Omagh. You'll find him eventually." The man peered over Sir Charles' shoulder, eyes darting around the room. The old man knew that look: it was the look of a man fighting against panic. He didn't want to push him too far. Not yet.

"Maybe we could meet somewhere else," he suggested. "I could buy you lunch. You've got to be hungry. A man can't live on Bushmills alone."

"I don't know, Charley. I don't know anything. I can't tell you anything."

"That's okay, Jimmy. Just for old time's sake, then. A couple of old friends talking about old times."

"Not sure we've got a lot to talk about, to be honest. They weren't exactly the good old days."

"Then we'll talk about the football."

The man's faced relaxed. "Sounds good," Jimmy said. "It's been a while since I had a decent meal, and El Tel has got your mob looking pretty tasty. Who knows, maybe you'll do it this time, home turf and all? Got to happen one of these days. So, if you're paying..."

"I'm paying. What do you fancy?"

"Steak. I'd love a steak. And onion rings. Can I have onion rings?"

"Of course you can, Jimmy. Anything you like." He just hoped that they could find a place that wouldn't turn Jimmy away, given the fact that he smelled as if he hadn't showered in a month. He looked worse. But with a little help he'd be able to stand. It was barely lunchtime.

"There's a place on the Old Kent Road I used to go to when I was younger, called Alfredo's. Of course Alfredo is long dead, but the place is still there. I bet they even have the same table cloths." There was a smile on his face, a twinkle in his eyes. There were memories there and that would get him to open up.

"I'm sure I can find it."

"I'll meet you there, though," Jimmy said. "Wouldn't want... you know..."

"Goes without saying," Sir Charles said. "See you at twelve?"

"Sounds good to me," Jimmy said, raising his glass. "*Sláinte.*"

# NINE

The car pulled up to a halt in front of the pub as Sir Charles reached the kerb.

Terry was about to get out of the car to open the door for him, but Sir Charles wasn't about to be waited on. He opened the door himself and stooped to slide inside.

"You're my driver, Terry, and if needed, a little extra muscle, but one thing you are not is my slave. I can open my own doors. I'm not helpless quite yet."

"Yes, sir. Sorry, sir."

"No need to apologise. It's fine. And you know what, you can drop the 'sir' every time you address me. I know it's ingrained, I know it's a recognition of rank, but I'm no longer a serving officer, so let's just settle on first names."

"Where now, sir?" the soldier said, completely ignoring the instruction.

"I'm not going to win, am I?"

"No, sir."

"Very well." Sir Charles glanced at his watch, aware that he had an hour to kill and the Old Kent Road was no more than ten minutes away, even at a London crawl. He wanted to get the smell of stale beer out of his lungs. There was a time when he would have found it comforting. Times change.

People change. Well, he did, at any rate. Jimmy Shannon, not so much. If Jimmy was going to make it to the restaurant on time he'd need to leave within the next ten minutes or so. He decided to wait, curious to see if the drunk intended to keep his promise or not.

"Where were you waiting for me?" Sir Charles asked Terry.

"There's a loading bay just a little way back there," the big man gestured over his shoulder with a hooked thumb. "My warrant card keeps the traffic wardens at bay. And for some reason lorry drivers don't seem to keen to start fights with me."

"I can't understand why," Sir Charles laughed. "Maybe it's because you're the size of a shed?"

"That does tend to act as a deterrent," Terry agreed.

"If you can drive around again, park in the same place, I'd like to hang around for a while. Call it a test of human nature. I'm meeting someone in the Old Kent Road at twelve. I suspect I'm about to be stood up, so best if he doesn't see me."

"Not a problem, sir," Terry said, pulling out into traffic. They moved at a slow but steady pace, just marginally quicker than the pedestrians, as they kept being brought up short by red lights. Sir Charles settled back into the depths of the leather upholstery and watched the world pass him by on the other side of the road.

It had been a while since he had been in this part of London. These streets belonged to a former life, one where his and O'Dwyer's lives had intersected. Coming back here had been a long shot, a very long shot, but judging by Jimmy's discomfort back there, maybe there was a thread to be picked at. He just needed to get Jimmy to talk, instead of drink.

"Any idea why someone would want to follow us?" Terry asked. His eyes were on the road ahead.

Sir Charles shifted in his seat before taking a look behind them, trying not to make it obvious that was what he was doing. He saw a dark blue Ford travelling a short distance behind them. The driver's face meant nothing to him. The tint of the rear window gave him the luxury of time to stare at the man.

"You sure he's interested in us?"

"It arrived while you were inside, parked ahead of me. It pulled out behind us as soon as we left. And now it's following us on our circle around."

Terry pulled out a small mobile phone and made a call, reading out the number plate.

"It's a hire car," he reported back. "We're contacting the hire company, see who's signed it out. Should have the answer in a few minutes. Want me to arrange to have him brought in?"

"No, it's fine. He's not doing any harm back there. Let me know when you find out more."

Terry pulled into the loading bay again.

The Ford slid past and drove beyond the pub before pulling to the side of the road.

"I could always wander over there, have a quiet word with the driver, sir?"

It was a tempting offer, but odds on the driver would be long gone before Terry was halfway across the street. Better to keep him in sight. Where was the leak? Not the security services; their lips were puckered up kissing each other's arses. So someone else had tipped them off. Either Jimmy, who was the obvious candidate, or the kid who'd slipped out of the bar as he'd ordered the Bushmills. And if it was he, then that meant someone was keeping an eye on Jimmy. That was an unexpected development.

"No need."

He was distracted from his thoughts by the sight of a man stumbling out through the pub doors and into the street.

There was no mistaking Jimmy Shannon's drunken swagger as he steadied himself against the pub wall. He stopped, took an exaggeratedly deep breath, and then set off away from them.

"Is that our man, sir?"

"It is indeed. There's no need to get too close. Let's give him a minute's head start."

The car in front showed no sign of moving as Jimmy staggered away, even though its engine was running. It seemed to be waiting for them to be the first to move.

"Give him a little longer," Sir Charles said. "He's heading in the right direction, so there's no need to spook him."

Jimmy turned an ankle as he walked, threatening to fall into the gutter, but somehow kept himself upright. He gave a glance at the floor as if to chastise the paving stones, and then looked up, staring in their direction without seeing them. It was an instinctive glance, left right left, the drunk determined to cross the road whether there was any traffic or not.

A car blared its horn as it sped along the road, missing him by a couple of inches. Its slipstream had his jacket blowing around him like Marilyn Monroe's white dress. Jimmy glowered after it, giving the driver a two-fingered salute. As Jimmy Shannon crossed the white line in the middle of the road, the car that had been tailing them was on the move, rubber screeching on tarmac as its tyres fought for traction.

"Shit," Sir Charles heard his driver say. He saw what was happening, but it was too late to do anything about it. Too late for Jimmy. The car peeled away from the curb into the middle of the road catching him hard in the centre of the bonnet. The impact tossed him into the air like a rag doll. He came down on the roof as the vehicle continued to gain speed, bouncing off it, all control stolen from his arms and legs as he flailed for a second before he hit the ground head first, blood and bone exposed through the ragged mop of hair.

He wouldn't be getting up again.

"Want me to go after them?" Terry asked.

It was the right response.

It was the only response.

Jimmy Shannon was a dead man. It didn't make a difference if they got out of the car and tried to help him or if they called for an ambulance. Unless he was the Second Coming he wouldn't be getting up again.

Still, he hesitated.

"Sir?"

"Call it in, they'll be looking for us. They can't get far."

# TEN

There was no doubt that Jimmy had been executed.

Maybe it hadn't been the original intention, but someone wanted to make sure that Jimmy only spilled his guts in a literal sense. That meant one thing, as far as Sir Charles was concerned; he knew something. That wouldn't help him now. The only possible upside was that they couldn't possibly know if Jimmy had talked. He needed to contain the situation quickly.

"Hello," he said, when his call was answered.

Terry was doing an efficient job of keeping the crowd back as the ambulance crew worked on, disregarding the fact that there were no signs of life.

They'd been issued strict instructions on how they were meant to play this out, just in case someone was still watching the events as they unfolded. As far as they were concerned, Jimmy was still alive and they were to make it look as though he was heading for Accident and Emergency.

It was all about keeping the pretense alive.

The longer that happened, the more control he had over the mess he'd just walked into. Jimmy's silence was worth killing for. Was it to someone from the present or the past? He needed to get himself to the hospital to ensure that the plan slowly forming in his mind had the chance of coming to fruition. He would have one shot at this. Once he played his hand, it was played. There was no calling those cards back. And right now, the trump was sitting behind the wheel of his car as they finally pulled away, following the ambulance as its siren cut a swathe through the traffic.

"Get us there ahead of the ambulance," he said.

The driver nodded and swung the car into an alleyway, flooring the accelerator, narrowly avoiding a stack of cardboard boxes piled at the rear of a restaurant.

At the far end of the alley traffic streamed past, but Terry slipped into it smoothly, without hesitation, despite the blaring horn and flashing headlights from a car forced to brake too sharply to avoid collision. Then they were back out on the main road.

Sir Charles glanced behind and saw the ambulance. There were a dozen cars between them, all of them slowing and pulling to the side of the road to allow it past. Terry had judged it perfectly. He surged ahead in the space that was being created, even though he received disapproving looks from drivers pulling to the side of the road to give the ambulance room to squeeze past.

"Nice work," said Sir Charles. The ambulance, wider than their own car, hadn't been able to negotiate the traffic at the same speed they had and was being forced to weave its way through well-meaning but sometimes thoughtless drivers, who didn't quite pull far enough to the side. Terry pushed the car through as traffic lights ahead turned red, barely avoiding a side-on collision with an idiot who'd jumped the lights from their left. Terry's focus didn't so much as flicker as he down-shifted and powered around the other car. Behind them, the siren continued to spiral as the junction filled with traffic unable to move out of the ambulance's way. Had it been a matter of life and death it would have almost certainly ended badly. The arteries of London weren't designed for saving lives.

"Drop me at the ambulance bay, then find somewhere to park," Sir Charles said, as the hospital came into sight. "Let me have your number and I'll call you when I need you."

"Sir."

Even as he slid out of the car, two ambulances followed them into the drop-off bay, and the siren of a third sounded above the noise of traffic.

Paramedics rushed with their charges to make sure that they got the medical attention they needed, handing them over with injury reports and as little fuss as possible. Orderlies were in position to take charge of Jimmy's body when it arrived. The mere mention of IRA involvement had been enough to get the hospital on side and keep the charade alive long enough to get the corpse in out of the cold.

They wheeled Jimmy's body into a side room while everything was put in place.

He made the call to Terry and waited while a man in a suit dismissed the rest of the staff.

"I've been told not to ask any questions," the man said when they were finally alone with Jimmy's corpse.

"That's probably for the best," Sir Charles replied, slipping his phone back into his pocket.

"What do you want me to do?"

"I need you to make it look as if this man is still alive."

"How long do you expect us to keep up the pretence?"

"A few hours at most. If they haven't made their move by then, we'll have time to make other arrangements."

"And you can guarantee my staff will not be at risk?"

It was a simple enough question.

Sir Charles wasn't sure that the man wanted to hear the truth.

How would it have helped to be told that there was every chance someone might come in to plant a bomb, so that it looked like a random act of terrorism rather than an attempt to silence one man? How would it have helped to say there was every chance a masked gunman would walk in through the front doors, firing indiscriminately? The only thing the administrator wanted to hear was that everything was going to be all right, that there was no risk.

Even if it wasn't the truth.

"There's no risk," Sir Charles replied. "Only my own man will be in the firing line. Trust me."

He regretted using the phrase almost as soon as it left his lips, but it was enough to reassure the man in the suit, who went about his work swiftly and efficiently. He set up an intravenous drip, taping the cannula to the man's skin without attempting to insert it into a vessel. The valve was closed so no liquid was going to leave the bag. He clearly understood that this was about creating an illusion that would at least stand up to a cursory inspection.

"What about the monitors?" Sir Charles asked.

"Hard to get an output from a dead man," the suit replied, but he started to attach the sensors to Jimmy's chest anyway. He then turned the machine so the screen couldn't be seen from the door and pressed a couple of buttons.

The machine began to emit a steady beep, imitating signs of life.

"How did you manage that?" Sir Charles asked, surprised and delighted with the depth of the illusion the man had created.

"I don't just push papers around all day," he said. "It's a test routine. The beep is confirming that there is a charge left in the internal battery."

"It would be good enough to fool me into believing the man's still alive, especially if I was concerned about being discovered. But sometimes it isn't the machines that give us away." Meaning the human factor. Loose lips cost lives.

"Anyone coming onto the ward will see someone on guard. They will talk, but not about it being a corpse."

"Perfect. Let word go round, high profile patient, vital to national security. That kind of rumour will help. But if you get enquiries from the press, stonewall them. The less ammunition we give them to use against us later, the better. I want people to think that they know something they are not supposed to."

"Understood. So what now?"

"Now we wait until someone makes a move. We're giving the enemy the opportunity to make a mistake."

The beeping had to continue long enough for the illusion to work.

Sir Charles had barely finished the cup of coffee that had been brought to him by an officious looking middle-aged woman when Terry arrived, dressed in a white coat that he'd liberated on his way through the hospital.

"Do we need to evacuate anyone?"

"Yes. But we can't. Not yet. Moving anyone will only tip our hand. We can't do anything that makes it look like this is a trap."

# ELEVEN

"Sir Charles," said the voice on the other end of the line. He took the call at the nurses' station. He caught the accent in those two words and recognised him as Dawson. "I wonder if we might have a word."

"Take 'patience': I'm not using it at the moment," Sir Charles replied, trusting the sarcasm wouldn't be lost on the desk-bound spook.

"We need to speak to you face-to-face."

"Again?"

"We've come into some additional information we feel is pertinent to your enquiry."

"Pertinent to my enquiry. Excellent, spit it out, man."

"It's not something I can discuss over the telephone, I'm afraid."

"How did you know where I was?" Sir Charles didn't need an answer. He was sure that Terry would be under strict instructions to keep his masters abreast of the day's events, even if they weren't in constant contact with him. As long as they didn't interfere, he didn't mind fulfilling their voyeuristic streak for a while. "On second thoughts, don't bother answering that. I know exactly how you know where I am. However, that doesn't change things. I'm in the middle of something here. I'm not at your beck and call."

"We are aware of the situation, Sir Charles."

"Then perhaps you'd allow me to get on with it?"

"Sorry, that's not going to happen. Indeed, the current predicament you find yourself in is precisely why we need to talk to you. Nothing's going to happen for the next half an hour."

It was a strange thing to say. How could the man be sure about that? Was he merely assuming that the wrong people didn't know where they were, or did he have a way into the ranks of the invisible enemy that didn't involve going through James Shannon.

"We'll meet you in the hospital chapel in ten minutes," Dawson said and hung up, leaving no room for argument.

Sir Charles handed the receiver back to the nurse who had continued with her paperwork at the station, oblivious to his presence. Was she the kind of nurse who would spread gossip about their new arrival?

There was only one way to find out.

Seeds sewn, he went in search of God.

There was a man standing outside the door of the chapel as he approached.

He apologised to a woman who tried to enter as Sir Charles walked towards him, but he stepped aside to allow the old man to step inside without a word. No names, no pack drill.

"Clearly, my reputation precedes me," Sir Charles said to the man as he entered. The agent's expression didn't so much as flicker. "Tough crowd," he continued, letting the door close behind him.

He'd expected there to be more than one person waiting inside the chapel for him. Maybe it was the way that Dawson had insisted on using the word 'we' instead of 'I'. Dawson sat alone in one of the pews, head bowed, seemingly in prayer. He didn't look up at the sound of the door closing. Sir Charles hadn't set foot in a hospital chapel before. The only salvation he needed was mortal in origin, not divine. He'd never felt the need to use religion as a crutch. Faith was interesting on an academic level, but not on a practical one. Even so, he'd expected there to be something more religious about the place, even if it were multi-denominational.

He took the seat next to Dawson and waited for the man to break the silence.

"Don't you find places like this strange?" Dawson said, eventually. "People come in here to escape the fears they have on the other side of that door, to beg and plead and bargain with the universe, but it's just a room, isn't it? There's nothing special about these four walls. There's no magic in here."

"You said this couldn't wait." Sir Charles said, not interested in a theological debate. There were things he needed to take care of.

"There's been a complication."

"Complication? You mean aside from my only lead being mown down in broad daylight? This business is complicated enough already."

The man pulled a file from his briefcase and slid a photograph out from inside. He placed it on the top of the folder and gave Sir Charles a moment to look at the man's face.

"Ronan Frost," he said eventually.

"Should I know him?"

"I certainly hope not. He's been undercover for over a year."

"One of your boys, then?"

"He's almost slipped off the radar, hasn't been in touch for months. He managed to get himself into an IRA cell here in London."

"And you think he's mixed up with this, somehow?"

"I don't think. I know. He's made contact."

"He has information?"

"More than that. He's been given the job of taking care of your guest."

Sir Charles thought about it for a moment. It was something he needed time to take in. "You trust him?"

"Why else would he call?"

"I've seen people who have gone native before: people who start off on one side, but end up on the other. Things change. People change."

"Not Frost."

"I admire your confidence," Sir Charles said.

"You have to let him succeed."

"I have to let him kill a dead man? That shouldn't be too difficult to arrange." He barked out a short laugh, entirely inappropriate, given their surroundings.

"If he fails, then all the groundwork he's laid will be for nothing. This is a pivotal moment for him. Blow his cover and his life's almost certainly over. These boys aren't forgiving. You know that."

Sir Charles didn't doubt it.

In an instant he was drawn back to a time when he'd lived with that same danger from day to day. It may have been half a lifetime ago, but the memories lingered. Living amongst the enemy when the slightest slip could prove fatal was the hardest job in the world.

"When is it happening?"

Dawson glanced at his watch. "Ten minutes."

"Thanks for the heads-up."

"He couldn't afford to put it off any longer. He'll be coming in at the start of visiting hours. There will be plenty of members of the public around. It has to look real."

"And that means taking my guard out, I assume?"

Dawson nodded.

It made sense.

Like he said, it had to look real. It was all about maintaining the illusion, even if it was a different trick to the one they'd started out with. Staff would be fielding questions from relatives, getting caught up in the general minutiae of health care, and stupid stuff like hunting down chairs for bedsides and vases for flowers. If they were lucky, they might even grab a couple of minutes to have a cup of tea themselves, hurriedly gulped down before it had the chance to go cold. It was the perfect time for someone to walk in and walk out unnoticed.

"Anything else?"

"We'll be in touch if there is."

"Of course you will."

Sir Charles gripped the back of the chair in front and rose, straightening his jacket before heading for the door.

The other man made no move to leave.

"Tell me something," Sir Charles said, one hand on the chapel door.

Dawson turned to face him.

"Your man, Frost. Was he driving?"

"I don't know," Dawson said, and for once Sir Charles believed him.

"Well God help him if he was, because I don't care what side you're on, you don't get away with murder in my world."

The other man didn't say anything for a moment. He simply turned to face the cross at the front of the room where there ought to have been an altar. "There is no God," Dawson said eventually.

"Oh, there is here, trust me, and he's a vengeful old bastard."

# TWELVE

"We've got a problem," Sir Charles said, as he returned to the side room.

He showed Terry the photograph he'd taken from Dawson. "Who's this?"

"This is the man who's going to kill our dead friend."

"Oh, right, and how's he going to do that? Raise him up only to take him down again?"

"Something like that."

"And I'm supposed to look the other way and let it happen?"

"You've got it. He'll be walking in here in the next few minutes to shoot our body."

"And I'm assuming you *don't* want me to grab him before he's done the job?"

"Not after, either." Sir Charles caught the look on the other man's face, but good soldier that he was, he didn't question his orders.

"You want me to follow him?"

"He's one of ours, on the inside. Orders from the top, we're playing the long game."

Terry nodded. "Very good, sir."

"I'll be inside the room when he gets here."

"Are you sure that's wise?"

"Let me worry about that. Just make sure no-one else comes in while he's there and that no-one tries to stop him when he leaves."

Terry paused for a moment. There was a time and a place for questions. This wasn't it. He nodded and looked up and down the corridor. "I'll hang around the nurse's station for a bit," he said eventually. "Good visibility. I'll be able to see people as they start to come in. It offers the best view of what's going on in the corridor, so anyone trying to stop our man on the way out will need to get through me."

It made sense.

Now Sir Charles just needed to hope that this Frost character wouldn't get trigger-happy when he saw him in the room.

It would all be instinct once he entered the room, no time for thought. If he saw Sir Charles as a threat, it would be just as easy to shoot him as well as the man in the bed, especially if he thought his life depended on it. The problem with an operative being deep undercover was quite simply that it was impossible to tell where his loyalties lay. If he couldn't snap out of the legend he'd made for himself, then Sir Charles would be facing an IRA operative, not a British soldier. It was a risk he was going to have to take. It might be the only chance he got to speak to the man.

He moved the chair into the corner of the room and closed the blinds. The room fell into near darkness. He sat in the chair, facing the door. With luck, Frost wouldn't immediately see him as he entered the room. Terry would ensure they were undisturbed.

He felt a curious sense of calm as he waited for the door to open.

The steady beep of the heart monitor sounded out the beat of the dead man's heart. He'd almost managed to put Jimmy's corpse out of his mind.

Then, under the beeps, he heard the soft click of the door opening.

"Hello, Ronan," he said after the man had closed the door silently behind him.

The shadow turned, gun in hand, drawn by his voice.

Frost swept the gun in his direction, but pulling the trigger wasn't instinctive. The movement was calm, not the whip of sudden panic. Ronan Frost was in control. That was good. It meant things were less likely to get messy.

"What are you?" Frost asked. Not who. What. An important distinction.

"A friend," he said.

"I don't have any friends," Frost said. "Not any more. I just have people I know. And I don't know you."

"You will soon enough, son."

"Someone told you I was coming."

"They did indeed."

"And you're going to try and stop me? Is that it?" Frost said.

"Not at all."

"Oh, right, you're just going to sit there while I shoot him then? I suppose you're going to let me walk out of here, too?"

"Of course I am. We're on the same side here, Mr. Frost. After all, that's why you rang ahead, isn't it? To make sure that no-one stopped you?"

"And yet you're here?"

"I needed a word, son. Simple as that. I need to know what O'Dwyer is doing over here on the mainland."

"O'Dwyer? As in Patrick?"

Sir Charles nodded. The gesture was lost in the darkness of the room.

"I didn't even know that he was here."

"But you've heard of him?"

"Of course I have, everyone has."

"And yet you didn't know that he was in the country? No-one's mentioned his name."

"I've said, haven't I?" The man's thick Belfast accent came out as he let himself get agitated.

"I need you to find out why he's here," Sir Charles said.

"I've already got a handler. I don't need another paymaster. Too many cooks."

He still hadn't lowered the gun, but he was holding it rather than threatening with it.

"Well, here's the reality of the situation, son. I'm the one who's sitting here, not your handler. And I'm telling you what I need."

He glanced across to the body lying on the bed and the machine beside it still beeping away in the imitation of life.

"I'm not your son," Frost said. "Stop calling me that."

"My apologies, Mr. Frost. No offense intended. Now, can I rely on you?"

"I can't promise anything."

"I wouldn't expect you to. Don't compromise your original mission. But if you hear anything, anything at all, I need to hear about it."

"How do I get hold of you?"

Sir Charles gave him the number for his club. Frost didn't write it down, just repeated it back to him.

"Henry will take a message. He is there day and night."

"Who do I say the message is for?"

"You don't."

"Not through the Service, then?"

He shook his head. "This is strictly off the books."

"Don't you trust them?"

"I don't know who I trust. I've been out of the loop for a while. Things have a habit of changing, especially allegiances. It's been quite a while since I was on the sharp end like yourself."

"I don't want your pity."

"I wasn't offering it."

Frost looked at the body once more then at his gun.

"I'll do what I can."

"Thank you," said Sir Charles.

Frost turned to leave.

"Aren't you forgetting something?" Sir Charles nodded towards the corpse on the bed. "If you don't do what you came here to do, there's no report in the papers, nothing on the news about the man killed in his bed. The wrong people are going to start to ask questions. You need to do your job, soldier."

The young man took a couple of steps towards the bed and raised the gun.

Sir Charles wondered how many men he had killed.

The silencer muffled the sound of the two shots that caused a couple of clouds of fibre to puff into the air. The steady *beep, beep, beep* of the machine mocked him. Frost pulled back the duvet to reveal the body, confirming that it was dead, but not understanding how Jimmy Shannon's heart could still be beating.

"He was dead before he reached the hospital," Sir Charles said.

"So this was a sting?"

Sir Charles nodded. "We were hoping to draw the enemy out."

"And here I am."

"I sincerely hope you are not the enemy, Mr. Frost."

But there was no escaping the fact that the undercover agent had shot at a helpless man not once, but twice, fully prepared to take his life to maintain his cover.

# THIRTEEN

"Bastard," Frost hissed the word under his breath when he was back in his car.

He slammed his hands against the steering wheel to release some of his anger. "Bastard. Bastard. Smug fuckin' bastard."

The man hadn't needed to do that.

He'd been testing him and he'd failed.

He could just as easily have told him that his target was already dead before he'd pumped the two bullets into his chest. But oh no, instead he had led him to the brink and pushed him over. Just a gentle push. A finger on the chest to help him on his way. He was every bit as fucked up as the men Frost was pretending to work with. The difference was, they had a cause. They had something they believed in. Did the smug old bastard in the chair believe in anything? Or was he one of them? A suit. Just doing his job. There was a difference. It was an important one.

He turned the key in the ignition and the engine roared into life.

He had no idea who he'd just faced, or how he fitted into what was going on. The man had talked like the Service. Five maybe. One of the higher ups. Not one of their front men, though. A puppet master. He was certainly pulling the strings. He'd have a plan for the body. His kind always did. He'd already used it to lure him out into the open, even if he hadn't known who would turn up to take care of Jimmy Shannon's loose lips.

A woman pushing a pram walked in front of the car just as it jerked forward.

He stopped inches away from it.

He hated women like that, who'd push their kids out into traffic first, happy to risk their kids' lives but not their own. He wanted to say something. To bitch her out.

She stared him down through the glass, making it absolutely clear she thought he was the idiot.

He knew that she was right, but maybe not in the way she thought.

He took a deep breath before looking around, checking there were no more surprises, little old ladies with bulging shopping bags or mini-Shearers or Cantonas at risk of being flattened, then pulled away again. Someone, somewhere, would want to know who had shot Jimmy Shannon, even if he'd already been dead when the bullets slammed home. CCTV footage was the bane of his existence. There was always a record somewhere. An angle. Someone would trawl through footage in search of clues. They'd see him. That was the point, of course. He needed the crew to trust him. But he didn't want his face plastered all over the Nine O'clock News.

Maybe this shady hospital visitor would pull a few strings to make things disappear, but he couldn't rely on it. There was always someone who couldn't resist picking at a loose end. Nothing was ever completely smooth, especially on a deep cover op. There was always a spanner waiting to be thrown in the works.

He gripped the steering wheel a little too tightly as he drove out of the car park.

The sound of an approaching siren set his heart racing. Frost breathed deeply, keeping his eyes to the front. Blue flashing lights moved closer through the traffic. Frost resisted the urge to weave his way through the cars. It was a hospital. Those lights belonged to an ambulance, not the police.

He needed to get a grip.

He settled into the traffic, as it started moving again, keeping a constant distance between his car and the car in front. No need to take any risks, or draw attention to himself by driving like an idiot. He put the radio on, the DJ promising a blast from the past and offering up a bland ballad meant to take his breath away. His orders were simple: go home and wait. Someone would contact him. He just had to keep his head down.

Frost knew how the Service worked.

That didn't change, even if the suit was operating outside the chain of command.

He would want to use the situation to his advantage.

It was always about working the angles with these people.

The suit had a single objective—hunting O'Dwyer. That meant he'd want Ronan to do everything he could to reinforce his position within the cell, cosy up to the top men and to hell with the risks. But that would afford him an air of protection, as well. If the press got hold of the fact that a patient had been shot while he was in hospital, they'd have a field day. It would turn into a witch-hunt, all the confirmation needed that an IRA cell was operating on the mainland, and then the fear mongering would set in. Conversely, if it were kept out of the papers, doubts about him would start to creep in. The situation needed to be managed.

The traffic started to thin as vehicles began to turn off the main drag.

Cars were moving at close to the speed limit, pedestrians going about their business completely oblivious to what was going on around them. They'd get home, see the news and realise how close they had been to the story.

Frost half-expected there to be someone waiting for him inside his flat.

There wasn't.

He checked the living room and the bathroom, moving through the place quickly, Browning in hand as he rushed from room to room, making sure it was clear. Old habits died harder than flesh and blood did. There was no sign that anyone had been in. Even if they had, if someone from the cell had spent the morning poking around in there, they wouldn't have turned up anything that would make him seem anything other than he claimed to be: a disaffected young Irishman fresh in the big city, unable to get work, unable to break the spiral.

The few things that linked him to the life he had led before he had successfully inveigled himself into the cell were hidden away beneath the floorboards. He had safeguards in place to confirm that the carpet hadn't been disturbed.

Even the names in the book beside the phone were made up. An entire identity had been invented for him before he had put himself out there and waited to be reeled in. His CO in 1 Para, Tony Denison, had called it a legend. A made-up life that was larger than any young man could possibly live. Denison had put him up for the job. Frost hadn't been sure at first. He wasn't some kind of spy. But he was a soldier, and that meant he went where he was sent, even if that was back to the Falls Road. It had been more than a year since he'd last answered to the name Ronan Frost. He had become Liam Murphy, body and soul.

It had been more than a year since he'd had any contact with family or friends. For all he knew, they might think he was dead. He had told them he was going away to work for a while without being able to tell them where or for how long, concocting a story about aid work in Africa where he might not be able to telephone and where they couldn't reach him. They wanted to believe him. That made it easier to lie to them.

It had taken him a month to make contact with the group, five more to become part of it. He hadn't had much of a plan at first beyond hanging around in the right kind of Irish bars, Republican ones with the tricolour hanging behind the bar. Then it was all about falling into conversation with the right men, saying the right kinds of things at the right time. Then there had been another six months of running errands, driving men with baseball bats so they could deliver a beating to someone who had said the wrong thing.

He saw a few faces, overheard a few names, but nothing worth breaking cover to report back. He was at the bottom of the totem pole, mixing it with the thugs who enjoyed violence and used the Cause as an excuse. There was no hint of anything grander happening behind the scenes. No echoes of Warrington, Brighton or Bishopsgate. But his silent paymasters were convinced something was afoot, so there was no coming in from the cold. Not until he had evidence that could make a difference.

He slipped the Browning into a cash bag stashed it at the back of the freezer box, behind a bag of frozen peas and a box of fish fingers, then put the kettle on.

The door opened without warning.

"Doesn't anyone knock any more?" he called out when he saw Lorcan Kelly making his way inside.

"Got something to hide, Liam?"

"Only my cock, mate. I could have been entertaining," he laughed. He knew that it sounded forced, but it was the kind of response Kelly expected. Everyone in Lorcan Kelly's world was afraid of Lorcan Kelly. The man had zero humour. Why should any other fucker have one?

"Well, Private, how did it go?"

Private. The man only ever called people by rank when they'd been accepted into the IRA. Calling themselves an army turned the struggle into a war in their eyes. And if it was a war, it wasn't terrorism. It was all semantics. But it worked. It fooled people in countries far enough away not to experience the fallout of their actions into treating them as freedom fighters that deserved their financial support. Hurray for the Boston Irish, financing murder for decades, he thought bitterly. One day what went on here would find its way all the back to that city, and they'd turn to the cameras and ask: *How could this happen to us?* What was the old adage? You got what you paid for.

"It's done," he said.

He couldn't bring himself to fake any kind of enthusiasm for killing, no matter what cause he was working for.

The man held his gaze for a moment, no change in his expression. He didn't say a word. It was as if those coal black eyes were looking deep inside Frost, judging him, sifting through his memories to be sure he was telling the truth. It was Frost who was the first to look away. He could have held Kelly's gaze longer, but too long, and a look became a challenge.

"Do you want the gun?"

"Of course I want the feckin' gun, you prick," Kelly snapped. "Why do you think I've been waiting outside this shitehole for you to come back?"

"Why didn't you stop me downstairs? You could have saved yourself the climb." His flat was on the eleventh floor of a tower block. The stairwell stank of piss and hopelessness and it had been a month since the lift last worked.

Kelly gabbed hold of Frost's lapels and pulled him close, his breath carrying the unmistakable odour of Guinness. "Just you remember who you're talking to, boy. You're *nothing*. You get that? You are *nobody*. I needed to be sure you weren't being followed. What kind of eejit are you?"

Frost resisted the temptation to speak. Even given the brownie points he'd banked in the hospital, a smart mouth was only going to encourage Lorcan Kelly to get a bit handy with his fists. Listen to Kelly, and he would say that he could have been as good as Barry McGuigan if he hadn't picked up the taste for stout. Having been on the receiving end of a few punches, Frost didn't doubt it for a minute. Kelly still carried himself like a fighter. He wore the scars of battle proudly.

"Sorry," Frost said.

"Better. Now what have you done with the gun?"

But even before Frost could tell him, Kelly had opened the fridge and squatted down so the icebox was at eye level.

"Behind the fish fingers, eh? You youngsters never cease to disappoint me. Good job that I followed you straight up here, isn't it? The pigs would have found this in seconds."

His voice mellowed, Kelly enjoying the opportunity to treat Frost like a child who needed to be shown the error of his ways.

"I thought it was a good place."

"And yet it was the first place I looked, eh? So how good was it, really? You would have been better stashing it under the spare tyre in your car than putting it in here, except even that pile of rust you drive would get stolen by the toe rags who hang around this shitehole. You really are going to have to get yourself a better place, Private. Or come stay at the squat. And take some feckin' pride in the way you live." He nodded at the washing up still in the bowl and the baked beans stuck to the bottom of the small pan on the cooker top. "You won't be doing much entertaining if you live like a pig. And you're a hero now. Act like one."

Kelly glanced at the box of fish fingers before putting them back into the freezer, and then tucked the moneybag containing the gun inside his jacket.

It was pretty obvious he was carrying. But that was the point. He was in advertising, like Saatchi and Saatchi. And the estate was the kind of place you didn't stick your nose into anyone else's business if you didn't want it to end up bloodied and broken.

"You've done us proud today, Private. I'll see you again in a day or so."

"So soon?"

"You make it sound like you don't want to see me."

"It's not that..."

"I'm only teasing you, big fella, it's good. It's all good. But we might have something big going down in the city, and now we know the stuff you're made of, we might just have a job for you."

"Whatever you need," Frost said. This was it. This was what he'd spent a year working towards. The door had opened. All it had taken were two bullets in a dead man's chest. Now he was on the fringe of something big. It had to be the same big thing that the suit had his knickers in a twist over. It was why O'Dwyer was over on the mainland. But he couldn't ask. One word out of place, and he'd find himself with that gun pressed up against his head.

"Good man."

Lorcan Kelly left, but Frost remained in the small kitchen for ten minutes, his hands shaking. It wasn't fear. Adrenalin surged through his system. It was happening. A couple of days was all that stood between him and getting his life back. He'd be quite happy to bury Liam Murphy once and for all.

# FOURTEEN

There was plenty of explaining to do, but Sir Charles had no intention of hanging around and trying to do it.

He wasn't the kind of man who responded well to misplaced authority, and there was none more misplaced than the one conferred on the plods of the Metropolitan Police, as far as he was concerned.

This wasn't his territory. He didn't have his hands on all of the strings he needed to be able to make the puppets dance. This was the kind of job for a man with contacts, a man who could make things happen, who could play the press at their own game. He didn't have to look far to find the right man for the job; he was still waiting for him in the chapel.

"It's done," Sir Charles said.

"And Frost?"

"Gone."

"No-one tried to stop him?"

"None of my people."

"Good."

"And only two people know that your man Frost shot a corpse."

"What about Saines?"

"Who?"

"Terry."

"He's standing guard outside the room. He hasn't been inside and has orders not to let anyone in until I return. The blinds are drawn."

"So you still want this to be kept hush-hush?"

"On the contrary. Now I want the information to be leaked to the press. I want you to make sure that you find CCTV footage that shows Frost entering the building and that you label him a known IRA sympathiser."

"I'm not going to sell him down the river. He's one of ours."

"You're not selling him down the river, you're cementing his place in the enemy hierarchy. Believe me. I know how this works. I've probably got a better idea than you do, for that matter."

That was enough to silence the man.

"The clip doesn't need to be clear. Nothing that will have his face on the front page of The Sun. All I want is for there to be enough substance to convince his IRA handlers that we know who did it, even if we can't identify them. They will know that the grainy figure is Frost, because they want to believe it's him. If you do your job properly, even his mother won't realise it's her son."

"Anything else?"

"Do you know where Frost is living?"

"Of course. He has a flat in a seedy estate north of the river. It matches the profile we created for him. Why?"

"I need you to keep a watch on his home. Once the papers start carrying the story, he'll be a rising star in their organisation. There will be a lot of comings and goings. Important people in the network. People we want to get our hands on. Your boys need to get photos of every single one of them."

"And you're thinking O'Dwyer will be one of them?"

"I'm thinking it's a strong possibility. It's a personality thing. He's a dominant personality. A natural leader. He can inspire people. If he has gone over to the other side, as you think, then imagine what it's like for the lowest person in the chain to have a personal visit from someone like him? That's how you inspire loyalty. That's how you get the man at the bottom to walk on hot coals in bare feet for you. Anything less than that, the grunts will do in a heartbeat, without an instant of thought."

"And that's why you think he's over here? To tell someone that they've done a good job?"

"Oh Christ, no. If Paddy O'Dwyer is back on the mainland, he's a man on a mission. And he's not the kind of man who'd ask anyone to do something he wouldn't be prepared to do himself. If he's here, he'll be at the heart of it, no matter what it is."

"So why would he risk everything by going to visit Frost? It doesn't make sense to me."

"That's because you don't think like a combatant, Mr. Dawson. You think like a desk clerk. But, to be fair, it could go down differently. He could arrange to have Frost taken to him at a safe house. If that's the case, there's a very good chance you'll not hear from your man again until the op's gone down. I'll be staying at my club, so I would appreciate it if you could get any pictures messengered over to me this evening. There may be some familiar faces in there."

The man raised an eyebrow, obviously surprised that Sir Charles thought he might recognise anyone close to the centre of things. "Who are you expecting?"

"Not expecting, but it wouldn't surprise me if O'Dwyer has kept in touch with a few people from the old days. When you trust someone with your life, you tend to turn to those same people for help when you need it."

"Even when they don't share your sympathies?"

"Trust has to be unconditional, Mr. Dawson. They may not have any idea what Paddy's involved in."

"Understood. So, if Frost leaves the flat with anyone else, you want us to follow him."

"If possible; but don't allow your men to compromise themselves. If O'Dwyer suspects we are close, he'll go to ground. If that happens, he'll double the steps he takes to keep himself hidden. Don't be surprised if the most interesting visitors come in the middle of the night."

"I know the drill," Dawson said.

"Good. I'll be speaking to someone who knows a little about computers. He's been developing something that, with luck, might help in us finding out what their target is."

"We've got people who can help on the technology side—" Dawson started.

Sir Charles raised a hand to silence him. "I'd rather keep it unofficial. The fewer people involved, the better. And, less chance of the situation being micro-managed from Whitehall."

He was going to work at his own speed, not have to sit on his hands waiting for clearance every step of the way. Better to beg forgiveness than ask permission. Besides, the man he had in mind was every bit as good as anything the Service was likely to be able to offer. Better.

"If I find that the software he's developing is likely to be of interest to your people, I'll suggest that he offers you an exclusive licence. Can't say fairer than that. I shall bid you *adieu*. The sooner we get the ball rolling, the better."

# FIFTEEN

Terry Saines went ahead to collect the car while Sir Charles stood outside the hospital entrance.

The last of the evening visitors were filing out. The reception would soon fall almost silent until the shift change.

While he waited, he used the mobile phone that felt uncomfortably large in the inside pocket of his jacket.

The call was answered on the third ring.

"Yeah?" the voice on the other end asked. It was no more or less than Sir Charles had expected.

"Philip?"

"Who else is going to answer the phone at this time of night? Who is this?"

"It's barely eight thirty," he replied.

"In the evening?"

"Yes, in the evening. And it's *Sir* Charles Wyndham."

"Oh, right," he said. Sir Charles could almost hear the man shuffling papers as if he didn't want whatever he had in front of him to be seen. "What can I do for you, Your Highness?"

"You know that's not what you're meant to call me, Philip."

"I do indeed, but it's more fun to rattle your chain. So?"

"I've got a proposition for you."

"I'm all ears."

"Not over the phone. Can we meet?"

"Where did you have in mind?"

"There's a restaurant a couple of streets from you. I can't remember its name...something Italian."

"Eleo's?"

"That's the place. See you there in half an hour? I'll stand you dinner."

"Make it forty-five minutes. I need to take a shower and get dressed."

"Do you want me to pick you up?"

"Probably best if you don't. Whatever car you're driving is going to stand out like a sore thumb around here. Don't want people talking. They'll think you're my sugar daddy."

"Heaven forbid. I'll see you there."

The phone fell silent as Terry pulled up in front of him.

In the distance, he could hear the sound of sirens approaching.

He felt a pang of guilt for misusing the goodwill of the NHS, knowing there were others who needed the help their stretched-thin resources offered. It didn't last. Something was going to happen, and soon, and it was going to test every one of those resources to the limit. It was a 'greater good' justification, but that was the kind of world he was operating in right now.

"You hungry?" he asked Terry as he slipped into the car.

"Wouldn't mind the chance to grab something," Terry said.

"How does a decent steak sound?"

"Like it'd hit the spot, sir."

He gave him directions.

There were only a handful of diners spread out over a couple of the tables. The waitress leant against the bar, flirting with the young barman, who was looking at the straining buttons of her too-tight blouse as he poured a drink. The décor was trattoria-chic, the same as a dozen other Italian restaurants in a five-mile radius. It was a slow night. The girl delivered the drinks to one of the tables then walked towards them.

"Evening, gentlemen. Do you have a reservation?" she asked.

"Sorry, no."

"That's okay, we're hardly drowning in bookings, as you can see. Table for two, is it?" She picked up a couple of menus as she passed the cash desk and started to show them towards a small table, with the prerequisite bottle of rosé dripping with candle wax, before he had the chance to respond.

"Three. We're waiting for someone else to join us."

She collected an extra menu, and then led them over to a table near the window.

"This okay for you?"

"Perfect," Sir Charles said.

Normally he would have picked a corner table, back to the wall, but this way he could keep an eye on the comings and goings outside.

"The man who's going to join us has, shall we say, a colourful past," Sir Charles explained to Terry, once the drinks were in front of them. He took a sip of the claret and tried not to wince at its harshness. "There might be things I want to discuss with him that you might think should not be discussed with anyone outside the Service."

"Do you trust him?"

"I do."

"Then that's good enough for me," Terry said. "You're the boss."

"That I am, Terry. And, I'd appreciate it if we kept this between us."

"Goes without saying, sir."

"Good man."

They didn't have to wait long for the third of their party to join them.

Sir Charles rose to greet him, a hand outstretched in welcome. The newcomer looked down at as if it was a snake coiled to bite. And maybe it was. After a moment's hesitation, he accepted it. He offered Terry, who had not moved, an uncertain nod, and then sat down.

"You didn't tell me that we were going to have company," he said.

"This is Terry. He's on the side of the angels, don't worry."

The man shrugged and picked up the menu. "If you're happy with him, then who am I to argue?"

"No-one," Terry said. Sir Charles raised an eyebrow, surprised at his man's tone.

Philip ignored him. "So this thing you wanted to talk to me about?"

"I need to know if it's possible."

"Now you've got my attention. Spill."

Sir Charles had rehearsed the request in his head, trying to find the delicate balance between revealing what was happening and tantalising Philip enough to hook him. Before he had the chance to speak, the waitress appeared at his elbow with her pad and pen in hand. She took their order and returned with a pint of lager for Philip. The other two were already well down their own drinks but declined the offer of another. Philip took a long draw then licked the froth from his upper lip.

"Needed that," he said then put the glass down, holding Sir Charles' gaze while he waited for an explanation. "You're very quiet, boss."

"Indeed. The last time we met you were talking about a computer program you were building that would take seemingly random facts, snippets of intelligence picked up out there, the shattering and the not-so shattering world events unfolding, and try to find connections among them?"

"Still working on it. The problem with the system is size. There are a dizzying number of possibilities. Everyone is adding to them every minute of every day, and any search involves rooting through a database the size of Harrods."

"I'm going to need you to sign the Official Secrets Act before I can tell you any of the details," Sir Charles said. "Once you've signed, you'll be caught up in the system. It will affect everything you do from that moment on..." The inference was obvious. Ask no questions and your life will be a whole lot less complicated.

The man shrugged as if to say 'easy come, easy go'. "Then best you don't tell me anything, because the only way that's happening is if you're steering the pen in my cold dead hand."

"We're talking about enough money to make you *very* comfortable. Not just beer and pizza comfortable."

"Island in the Pacific?"

"Not quite. Isle of Dogs, perhaps."

Philip took another pull at his drink. Sir Charles recognised the sign. He was considering it, but needed to be doing something at the same time.

"Go on then," he said. "I'm game, but we're talking penthouse flat in the new developments."

"You heard that, didn't you, Terry? Philip has promised not to ask any questions that might be construed to go against or interfere with national interest, and has, as such, opted to accept our word that we are acting on Her Majesty's behalf, and that he really doesn't want to know what's going on."

"Sounds about right, sir. I'm sure that if Phil here says that he's not going to ask any difficult questions or go rooting around where he shouldn't, he won't."

Philip gave him a look, though barely moving his head.

"Philip," he said. "Not Phil."

"Ah, sorry," said Terry. "Philip."

"Good," Sir Charles said, acting as if the business part of the evening was concluded. Now, down to work. "The program you talked about. Could it, for instance, draw up a list of the locations of the highest concentrations of people in the city at a given time on any given day, the locations of events that are due to take place on that day, transport connections, that kind of thing, and make sense of them in some way?"

"Make sense how, exactly? What are you thinking?"

"Join the dots. Identify key locations where more than one of these conditions exists?"

Philip shrugged. "Identify intersections? Of course. If you've got all the raw data input, then it's a fairly straightforward process to analyse it. The hard part is putting the data together in the first place. How big an area are we talking about?"

"Greater London."

Philip shook his head. "You'd need an army of trained monkeys. Seriously. Do you have any idea how many people there are passing through the city in any given twenty-four-hour period? You're talking a population of getting on for seven million, and that's not counting the transients. In terms of events, there are literally hundreds of thousands, from poxy little fêtes to grand galas, parliamentary gatherings, protest marches, football matches, concerts, you name it. How quickly would you need your answers?"

"Realistically, twenty-four hours, forty-eight at best, but even then it might be too late."

"Then this isn't the way to do it. Yes, I can put the program together in a couple of days, but it's going to take a month to get all the data you'd need for any meaningful results into the system. It just doesn't all exist in one place."

"Actually, it might," Sir Charles said, thinking on his feet.

# SIXTEEN

"MI5? You're going to let me into the MI5 system? And I'm not signing the OSA? Yeah, I can see that flying with the top brass." The young man rocked his chair back onto two legs and, shaking his head in disbelief, laughed loud enough to make the other diners look their way. "What? Is it Christmas?"

He dropped the chair back down onto four legs again and slumped back into the seat.

A slow smile started to appear on the younger man's face, as if he'd reached a possible answer for himself.

"I'm right, aren't I? Oh my fucking lord. Love it. You are one mad bastard, Charley. This is a joke, isn't it?"

"No."

"You're serious?"

"Deadly."

"Shit. You're telling me you'd let someone who's spent the last three years at Her Majesty's Pleasure loose on the nation's most secure computer system?"

"Needs must."

"I love you, Charley. I absolutely fucking love you. Fucking crazy. You want someone who thinks like a criminal balls deep in the best fucking computer network in the land. Brilliant."

Sir Charles had been impressed by the man when he had first met him. More so now. And he had to admit; he rather liked the idea of telling those two suits who'd conscripted him into this whole mess that he intended to set their worst technological nightmare loose inside their system. "It takes a thief to catch a thief."

"You really are one devious old bastard, Charley, you know that?"

"It has been said before. So, are you interested?"

"Excellent. I'm in. What do you need me to do? The practicalities?"

"This goes no further," he said, "There's a credible IRA threat of an attack on the mainland. We need to be ready for it."

Philip leaned forward, stretching across the table and almost overturning his drink.

"The IRA? Fuck me. The IR fucking A? This is mad."

"Don't worry, you won't be in any danger—"

"What planet are you on, Charley?"

"Fine. You're the best man for the job. That means I'm willing to gamble people's lives on you."

"Don't put that shit on me. This isn't fair."

"I never said it would be, Philip. I only said you'd be well paid."

He shook his head. "Jesus, I'm going to regret this. I know I am. But I'm in."

# SEVENTEEN

*The man lay on the bed, a red blossom spreading across the pure white sheet covering his chest. Beside him a machine emitted an unchanged beep, beep, beep. He hadn't killed him. He'd shot him in the heart twice, but he was still alive.*

*Frost raised the gun and fired again, the sound impossibly loud despite the silencer attached to the weapon.*

*He fired again and again, long after he should have run out of ammunition.*

*The pool of blood continued to spread, seeping down into the mattress around the dead-not-dead man, until the sheet was stained red. Still, the machine issued its taunt: beep, beep, beep.*

*His finger squeezed down on the trigger again and again, willing the machine to fall silent.*

*There were no more shots to be fired.*

*There was nothing more he could do.*

*The body on the bed opened its eyes.*

*It stared up at him.*

*Frost's heart raced. It pounded against his ribs until he could feel it swelling, fit to burst. The corpse's mouth opened, but no words came out. All that bubbled from the dead-not-dead man's lips was blood so dark that it was almost black. It spilled over his chin. Deep down inside his throat, the dead-not-dead man gurgled as the viscous fluid escaped.*

Frost sat up, screaming.

It wasn't the first time he'd seen death close up. It wasn't even the first time he'd been the one to pull the trigger and help a man die. But something felt different about what he had done at the hospital. The world of good and evil was split by fine hairs. Now the echo of the machine stuck inside his head and refused to be dislodged. It was the sound of his own, personal ghost.

Sweat clung to his skin and glued the sheets to his naked body.

In the moments that followed the realisation, he'd been tangled up in a nightmare. The draughts chilled the sweat on his skin, sending a shiver chasing down the ladder of his spine. He fell back onto the bed, breathing in deeply, holding the air in his lungs for a count of five before letting it leak out through pursed lips. He had been doing this for too long. He wanted his old life back. He wanted to be Ronan Frost again. He hated who he had been forced to become. Liam Murphy wasn't who he was. Liam Murphy was a construct of his imagination, the deepest, darkest parts of who he could have been. Liam Murphy was a bastard. A dangerous bastard.

He looked at the clock on the nightstand.

The second hand moved slowly, reflective paint making it glow in the dark.

He could have watched it tick slowly around the clock face for hours if it meant he was counting out the seconds before this other—more real—nightmare came to an end.

There had been times when he'd been tempted to walk away, and not just because it seemed to be taking forever to get anywhere. Now he wished that he had, because this close to his destination, he realised he was lost. Metaphysically. Psychologically. Spiritually. Ronan Frost was lost, even if Liam Murphy knew exactly where he was. He had no way of knowing if Frost would ever find his way back, and if he did, how much being Liam Murphy would change him.

The one truth he could not escape was that, no matter what happened next, being Liam Murphy meant that Ronan Frost could never be the same again.

His mouth tasted of stale whiskey.

He had needed a couple of glasses to take the edge off. It was the only way he got to sleep at the moment. He knew it wasn't healthy, but it was part of the new persona. Part of fitting in. Being one of them.

He lifted his head off the pillow again, painfully aware of the throbbing inside his skull, the bones too small to contain its contents.

It was barely five thirty.

He wasn't going to be able to sleep.

He swung his legs around and stumbled out of bed in search of a glass of water and painkillers.

From the kitchenette window he could see the moon. It would be a few hours before the sun rose above the cluster of tower blocks in the distance. He had a view that stretched out across familiar parts of London and, in time, would catch the sun glinting from the dome of St Paul's. He rinsed a glass out and filled it with water from the tap. It tasted stale. The water fed the whole of the block and had been standing in the pipes for too long to feel fresh. He threw back a couple of paracetamol and washed them down with tepid water.

If the call came today, they would see what a wreck he was.

That might not be a bad thing when it came to saving his soul, but for Liam Murphy it would be a disaster.

He splashed water over his face.

It didn't help.

Frost opened the door out onto the walkway and stood on the threshold, feeling the near-freezing night air on his skin. There was no sign of anyone moving in any of the other flats. He stepped out to the rail wearing nothing but his boxer shorts.

A cat gave a screech and shot out from the shadows somewhere beneath him, pursued by another that leapt from the dustbins, sending a lid clattering to the ground. Until that moment, the night had been silent, not even troubled by the distant hum of traffic that underpinned the symphony of London.

Something caught his eye.

He looked down at the parking area below the flats.

A single, tiny red dot that he almost missed the first time.

He kept his gaze fixed on the spot, scanning the darkness for the tiny red flare of light.

There.

It was the glow of a cigarette.

Someone was sitting inside one of the parked cars, smoking while they watched and waited.

It was too dark to be able to see whether it was a man or a woman, or even make out the model of the car. It was a strange time to be enjoying a drag on an Embassy Regal. He thought about going down to check it out, but that was something Ronan Frost would do, not Liam Murphy. Instead, he ducked back inside the flat, determined to try and find another couple of hours' worth of sleep.

Instead he lay in the sweat-soaked sheets, staring up at the Artex whorls and stipples across the ceiling, watching the landscape change as the shadows stretched out with the rising sun. He couldn't sleep because he knew they were watching him. Whoever they were.

That was the problem with being caught in the middle, with no idea which side trusted you the least.

# EIGHTEEN

Philip had given him a list of the kit that he was going to need to bring his idea to fruition.

It didn't mean a lot to Sir Charles, but looking at the list of prices against the list of specs, it was a fair assumption that the hacker was chancing his arm with some of his requests. It wasn't Sir Charles' money, so he didn't particularly care, but the fact that the two computers alone were a couple of thousand pounds each was mindboggling. He had no idea of what most of the equipment was supposed to do, and a few thousand pounds here or there was just a splash in the ocean. It gave him something to focus on. He needed that. His meeting with Dawson's man, Frost, concerned him.

He hadn't expected him to pull the trigger before being told Jimmy Shannon was already dead.

He wasn't sure what that told him about Frost, but it certainly said something.

Even after he'd finished dictating the list, Philip had said that there was other stuff he needed, bits and pieces of software he could get hold of from a network of likeminded friends—which was a polite euphemism if ever he'd heard one—he worked with online.

Sir Charles did what he was supposed to do; he nodded in all of the right places, even if it made less sense than ancient Greek to him.

"I'll be honest with you, Charley: the world has moved on a long way while I was away—frighteningly so—and it's taking a while to catch up. But I won't let you down."

"I have absolute faith in you, Philip."

"Thing is, if I'm going to do this, I'll need new equipment to work with. My rig is pretty dated now, and, honestly, I don't want hand-me-downs that MI5 think they can spare. No telling what spyware they'll front-load them with, thinking they're being clever. I wouldn't ask, but you know, national security and all that."

"Don't worry," he had said. "I'll take care of it."

And he had meant it.

He *was* going to make this work. Somehow. Even if the world had moved on.

This wasn't just about people on the ground gathering information; it was about piecing it all together, trying to see patterns in the raw data. This was about the thought-processes an experienced operative would have, and how their very human brains would make those connections and logical leaps despite the sheer volume of detail involved. This was about finding a way to bridge the gap between man and machine. Not so long ago, it would have taken a week to get a computer to process the movements of a terrorist and search through the airline databases to find out if they had entered or exited the country. Now, that kind of search took minutes. The sheer volume of detail that was coming in from all over the world would be far too complex to be dealt with by analysts with index cards and maps and pieces of string, who relied on remembering what might be recorded in a file that had not been touched for more than a year. That was a skill that took a lifetime to develop and couldn't be passed on to the next in line, but a machine could be trained in it, surely? That was Sir Charles's gamble, here: that a machine could offer something more permanent, something that wouldn't miss the slightest detail in its search. In other words, something better.

First, though, he needed to convince the people at MI5 that employing an ex-con was in fact a stroke of genius.

That had been last night.

In the cold light of morning, those promises seemed much harder to keep, but, then, weren't so many promises made in bed just like that?

He could hear the sound of movement in the corridor outside his room. That meant it wasn't too early to give his man in the Service a call. Dawson sounded far too bright and breezy to have just woken up. In point of fact, he sounded positively chipper.

"Sir Charles. Good morning."

"Nice to know I'm not the only one hard at work already," he lied. He hated the idea of the other man working when he was lying in bed, but until they made videophones, he wasn't about to confess he was tucked up nice and warm.

"We had a team in place by sunset," the man said, clearly assuming that Sir Charles had rung in for an update on their surveillance of Frost. "Our man hasn't received any visitors since then, but he did appear on the balcony of his flat before sunrise wearing nothing but his underwear."

"Does he know we're out there?"

"Hard to say, but I don't think so."

"Because if he did, he'd have wandered out naked," Sir Charles said.

"Ah, I forgot you'd met him. Yes, exactly. He'd have sent us a nice message. That's his style."

"Keep me up to speed. While I've got you, I need a favour. I need access to the MI5 database and its links to other agencies."

There was a moment of silence on the other end.

The request had caught the man off guard.

It wasn't a big ask.

It was a huge one.

"I'm sure that I can arrange to have an operative available, but perhaps you can tell me what other agencies you need to link to? There are protocols we'll need to follow before we can access certain data."

Red tape.

Miles and miles of glorious red tape.

He knew that if he tried to get Philip inside MI5 there would be a million annoying little restrictions used to handcuff him, meaning he couldn't work freely. It wasn't going to work. He'd end up spending his life tilting at cyber-windmills if he wasn't careful. He needed a new plan of attack.

"Remind me, I'm cleared to access the system?"

"You are indeed, Sir Charles, though as I am sure you can appreciate, we are talking about an incredibly sophisticated system. It would take months of training to get you up to speed operating it. It's a much better use of resources to have one of our operators use it on your behalf."

"I'm sure it is. However, I'll be there in an hour. If I'm going to need one of your operators to hold my hand, make sure he's got his backside in the chair and is waiting for me when I arrive."

He could almost hear the sigh of relief from the other end of the line.

He was banking on the operator assuming he was just another late-middle-aged man who didn't have a clue about how things worked. He wouldn't be too far wrong, but the more he played up to it, the easier it would be to get what he wanted.

"I'm sure we'll be able to accommodate you. I'll arrange to have a car collect you."

"No need. Just make sure that Terry knows I will need him for a few more days."

He hung up.

A knock on the door indicated that the breakfast tray he had ordered was ready for him. He showered, and dressed as he ate, mentally making a list of the jobs he needed to take care of before he arrived at MI5.

There were always two directions to attack a problem from, and, in this case, his solution ought to provide Philip with the access he needed and the work hours he preferred.

He checked his watch.

Seven thirty.

Still early, but he knew that Philip was a night owl who'd turned day and night upside down. He'd be going to sleep in a few hours. Sir Charles pulled up his number and made the call. The young hacker sounded far more alive than he had the night before.

"Last call for requisitions, my man," he said once they'd exchanged the usual pleasantries. Every time he spoke to the hacker, he found himself liking the young man more, despite his background, or perhaps because of it. If the Service had spotted his talent before any latent criminality took hold, he would almost certainly been working for the government, not against it.

"I'm good. Unless you've got one of those time-twisters that could make the day a bit longer, because time's the thing we need now." Philip laughed, but there was an edge of nervousness in it. It might have been a mistaken to tell the hacker exactly what the consequences of failure were. It was a heavy burden to put on his young shoulders. But he was banking on the fact that Philip would rise to the challenge, and that was down to a basic reading of personality types. Sir Charles knew people. He'd stake his life on just how well he could read them. He'd also stake the lives of thousands of Londoners.

"I'm ahead of the game," Philip promised. "I've called in a few favours, got my hands on some of the software I need, including an algorithm I think is going to make all the difference—if I can get it to work. The guy I got it off would shit a brick if he knew how it was going to be used, mind you."

"Excellent. I'm making a call now to be sure all of your equipment will be with you inside the hour."

"Do you have any idea what the time is? You're not going to be able to get anything at this time in the morning."

"Of course I am," Sir Charles said. "It may be 1996, and the world has changed a lot in the last hundred years, but I'll let you into a little secret, Philip: a title still gets you certain privileges. One of those is being able to get hold of someone who can arrange just about anything to be put on board a delivery van, at any time of day or night."

"Man, the aristocracy have really got it made, haven't they? Silver spoons and all. Are you sure your posh drivers will be able to find my little slice of the ghetto?"

"He'll be paid very handsomely to risk venturing that far north of the river, Philip. I'm sure everything will be fine.

He knows which side his bread is buttered. Metaphorically speaking, of course."

"Should I be tugging my forelock, Charley?"

"Not at all. I'm more concerned about you doing the job you're being paid for. That's all that matters to me, not your social standing."

"Speaking of which, what's the plan? Do I need to get suited and booted for our visit to the MI5 building? Not that I actually know which building they are in."

"No need, I'm making arrangements to work from the comfort of your own home."

"How on earth are you pulling that little feat off?"

"That knowledge is above your pay grade, Philip."

"Understood, boss."

# NINETEEN

Frost was woken for the second time in a few hours, this time from a nightmare-free sleep.

He didn't feel any better for it.

A woman shouted at her children in the flat above him, the ceiling paper-thin. The rumble of a neighbour's electrical appliances tormented him as they came on and off. By a trick of the building's acoustics, the noise travelled as if his flat was the sound box of a musical instrument, meaning it was louder inside his apartment than it was in theirs. Or, at least, that's the way it felt to him.

The light that crept in through the windows was thin and wintry. It struggled to penetrate the nicotine-stained net curtains that had been hanging at the windows long before he'd taken up residency.

He had no plans for the rest of the day. It already felt a lot longer than it needed to be. He was living in that anxious zone between expectancy and solitude; someone *might* be coming knocking today, they might not. Maybe tomorrow. Maybe they just wouldn't show up. Maybe he'd watch the news and hear about what Lorcan's boys had been up to and this would be as close as he ever got to the action. The man had said a couple of days, but plans could change. The man of the hour could easily become yesterday's hero overnight.

Today he needed to serve his other masters.

Making the mental switch was going to be hard.

But if there was word out on the grapevine, he needed to hear it. They needed to hear it. Something was about to go down, that much was obvious. But what, where, when? Lots of variables with no answers. Another variable hung over his own involvement.

Doors started to slam, the clamour of children's voices rose out on the walkway, the little bastards herded out of the flats and sent on their way to school. Not that most of them would arrive there. The estate kept the truant officer busy.

It had taken him a long time to get used to sleeping in a place like this, waking up in the middle of the night longing for home, wishing he were anywhere else but here, anyone else but him.

But now he could block it all out.

This place wasn't real.

Not *really* real.

It was a story. A made-up place for a make-believe man.

It only existed while he was doing the job. When it was over, the estate would melt into nothing and he could forget all about it. Forget everything he had seen and heard in the stairwells and walkways.

As a god-fearing Irishman, he had a pretty good definition of hell, and this was it.

The pipes banged as he turned the tap to pour himself a fresh glass of water. Someone slouched past the window as he gulped it down. The silhouette didn't linger long enough for him to see who it was.

It caught his eye because whoever it was had come from the wrong direction to have come from the stairwell, meaning they'd exited one of the other flats along his landing. They weren't coming to see him. That didn't stop his hands from shaking. Frost wanted this over. The best and worst thing that could happen to him, he realised, was for a stranger to arrive at his door with the message that it was time. A month ago, it had been the constant fear that the next knock on the door heralded discovery, and promised him being bundled into the back of a van and driven out into Epping Forest to visit a shallow grave. He wouldn't be the first to be taken out there.

No-one knocked.

No-one walked in uninvited.

An hour later, he was itching to get out of the flat.

He signed on for his unemployment benefit every fortnight, just like everyone else, standing in the line, head down, dispirited, then staring at the jobs board pretending to look interested in offers of telesales and building work. The ritual meant he fit in with the people who lived around him. The few that worked did so in fits and starts, picking up jobs off the books, paid cash-in-hand so they could still claim their government handouts. Being unemployed wasn't a bad thing in a place like this; it was just a way of life, which was so much sadder on every level. The estate was easy prey for the loan sharks and creditors promising buy now, pay later, only to come around knocking with their collection book every Friday. Plenty of them came with a baseball bat. Having spent a year on the estate, Frost wondered if that was to threaten the reluctant debtors or to defend themselves against the army of kids.

Frost's bank account and savings weren't out of reach to Liam Murphy, but he couldn't risk being seen to be living beyond his means. Questions would be the death of him. That meant going out, hitting the streets, trying to pick up grunt work: hod carrying, the occasional bit of heavy work for one of the loan sharks, anything that would get him in closer with the Irish and put a few quid in his pocket. A man couldn't live on fifty-five quid a week in this city. He just couldn't.

Frost left the building and crossed the quad towards the alley that would take him down towards the distant river, Holborn, and the roads that led across it into the city. He had almost forgotten about the car he had seen in the middle of the night. All that remained was a collection of cigarette butts that had been thrown from the driver's window. They made a pattern on the ground. So it hadn't been a dream. He kicked them with his toe, scattering them, then gave a glance around to see if there was anyone acting out of the ordinary.

Watching.

It didn't take him long to spot another man in a car across the quad, sitting there seemingly engrossed in the morning's newspaper.

This wasn't the kind of place you parked up to skim the headlines unless you were waiting for someone.

He was tempted to go over and tap on his window.

Tempted, but not stupid.

Instead he strode out in the direction of the newsagents to pick up the morning edition, and then made his way towards the local pub to join the early morning drinkers and pretend to look for a job while he waited for something to happen.

It would pass the time.

And if he got lucky and the right people came in, who knew what he might hear?

O'Dwyer's name for one thing.

It was as close to a plan as he'd had for the time being.

The bar was heavy with the reek of stale smoke. No amount of polish could ever completely mask it. Not that the landlord was particularly handy with the duster.

The man behind the bar looked up as he walked in with his newspaper tucked under his arm.

"We're not serving yet, squire," he said.

Frost glanced at the clock behind the bar. It was five minutes short of eleven o'clock, the magic hour when places like this started to come alive.

"No worries," he said, looking around. There were already a couple of men sitting at tables, their pound coins on the bar, waiting for the moment the first pint could be pulled.

Even though it was the middle of the morning and the Met had better things to be doing with its time, there was always the possibility a policeman might stick his head in through the open door; but with no alcohol on the table, no licensing laws were being broken.

Frost held up his own newspaper to show that he had the same thing in mind.

"Be my guest," the barman said.

He put a few coins on the counter. "Put a Guinness in the pump for me."

"Will do." The barman didn't touch the money.

The other men didn't look up from the racing form. One made a note on where his dole money was destined to be lost with a tiny blue pen he'd stolen from the bookies across the street.

In a way it was a haven, a place of normality far from the grim life outside, where people left each other alone with their thoughts.

Frost scanned the jobs page and picked out a couple of vacancies for drivers and circled them, just in case anyone picked up his paper later to see what he had been doing. It was all about the illusion. It needed to be real to be sold. He pulled a handful of coins from his pocket and went over to the payphone to feed the slot and call after one of the driving jobs, just loud enough to be heard, giving them his home number, and thanking them for their time. He hung up as Con O'Toole came through the door.

"You're early," O'Toole said, leaning on the bar. He ordered a stout then came over to join Frost at his table, no respecter of the code of silence, bringing Frost's drink over with him.

Another couple of men stumbled into the bar from outside, filling the air with laughter for a moment. It was enough to lift the heads of two of the old men from the racing form, just long enough to show their disapproval.

"Nowhere better to be," Frost said, putting his newspaper down on the table.

"Picked any winners?" O'Toole asked, glancing at the paper. But he seemed to lose interest when he saw that it wasn't open at the racing pages.

"I only ever back the long shots," Frost said.

"Ah, lad, there's no jobs out there for likes of us. Not unless you're willing to break your back to get on the building sites. And even then, there's some that don't like the way we talk."

"You're not wrong there. Besides, that'd mean investing in an alarm clock," Frost laughed. "I really don't fancy having to learn how to get up in the morning again."

"None of us want that now, do we? Anyways, you still haven't told me what you're doing here so early. It's not like you. Woman trouble? Tell me it's woman trouble. I could do with a laugh at your expense, laddy."

Frost took a look around the room.

There were close on a dozen men in the bar now, and at least half of them were well over sixty. They didn't look particularly henpecked.

"Lack of woman trouble more like," he said.

"Ah, yes. Sadly, that's a state of affairs I'm all too familiar with, but you're a good-looking lad. You should be taking some drunken lassie up to your place every night. You know the deal, give 'em a drink, ask 'em if they've got a bit of Irish in 'em, and if they say no, ask 'em if they'd like a bit of Irish in 'em. Easy." O'Toole finished off his pint in one long, slow chug. He waggled the glass at Frost.

"Hah, if only, man, if only," Frost said getting to his feet, getting the message. "Same again?"

O'Toole nodded.

Frost called, "Two more," to the barman as he walked towards him.

"Now you know the other reason he's called Con," the barman said, with a smile. "He could come in here potless and drink himself blind, people happy to finance his addiction."

"Poor sod. I feel sorry for him."

"Course you do, everybody does. That's the card he plays. And he's good at it. Never gets anyone to buy him more than a pint day; you have to remember, I watch him do this every day. Before he's finished this pint, he'll have picked up the next sucker and the next and the next, then he'll stagger off home to sleep it off."

"Not much of a life is it?"

"Ah, bigger tragedy: old Con used to be someone once upon a time."

"Did he?"

The man placed the first pint on the bar to let the head settle, then tapped the side of his nose. "Used to be quite the Big Man back home, if you know what I mean."

"I had no idea," Frost said, surprised that the barman would confide in him so readily. But then, it had been here the cell had first approached him, and most likely the barman was connected, so he would have heard about Frost's adventures yesterday. He'd know who was on the inside and who was out, who could be trusted and who was just a regular punter.

"He's harmless enough," the barman said. "But if you get him talking about the old days, believe me, he'll talk the hind legs off a donkey."

Without Frost even noticing, the man had poured the second pint and topped them both up once the heads had settled. No short measures. He nodded and settled up, carrying the drinks back to the table. Before he reached his seat, the barman had turned the music on. He put one of the pints down in front of Con O'Toole.

"You're a scholar, sir," the man said, raising the glass in salute before taking a sip. "A gent and a scholar. Proper Irish."

"Pleasure," Frost replied.

"And this, laddy, this is the fine tune, right out of the old country," O'Toole said, tipping his head to one side as if to hear the music better. The sound of the Dubliners performing their version of 'I'm a Rover' played over the sound system as his feet tapped time with the track. It was a bloody mawkish song. Frost had never quite got behind the Irishman abroad thing, where everything from back home was suddenly a hundred times better and more important. It just wasn't. And if he had to listen to another man butchering The Cranberries he'd happily knock him out. He'd only need one punch if the joker was wet enough to know the words.

"I'm a rover, seldom sober," he joined in. He couldn't carry a tune. "I'm a rover of high degree."

A couple of the old men looked in his direction and smiled.

Frost guessed that they must know Con pretty well, and were expecting to be tapped up for the next drink. A few more guys had filed in. A couple of the younger men at the bar looked like they were about to say something, right up until they got a look from the barman. Con was obviously part of the fixtures and fittings, more than just tolerated, liked and maybe even respected after a fashion. In any other bar, an old drunk would have been given short shrift. Even a happy old drunk.

"It could be your song, Con," Frost said, offering a slight smile.

"It certainly could."

"So, I've always wondered, what brought you over here?"

"Ah, there's only so much you can do to make things change if you sit on your arse," he laughed. "Sometimes you have to go out to where the action is and *do* something to change the world." It was a grand old impassioned speech. There was a sudden light behind his eyes that had been missing right up until that moment, as if a memory was fighting its way through the alcohol fog. The barman had been on the money. Even without him saying another word, Frost knew precisely what he was saying.

"Wasn't there stuff to be done over there?" Frost said.

He didn't want to use the word Ireland.

They both knew what they were talking about.

Only idiots drew attention to the Troubles if they didn't want to grandstand it. He wasn't an idiot. He didn't want the wrong people noticing him. He wanted the right ones paying attention. That meant he had to be clever.

There were words that caught the attention, even now. Words that caused anger, suspicion, fear and resentment in the general public, but another emotion in those on the inside: people who were afraid that they might be dragged out into the light before they were ready. People who had seen the injustice of the Guildford Four and the Birmingham Six and the Maguire Seven. Even if the verdicts had been quashed, they knew the beat-down that preceded it, and the pain. There was no glory in being like Bobby Sands. No matter how the recruiters from the cells spun it, dying in prison because you'd starved yourself to death was not the way most young Irishmen dreamed of going.

Not that they ever saw themselves as anything other than freedom fighters.

It was all about casting off the yoke of English oppression.

Sometimes it was a fault of the British government; sometimes it was factions amongst their own people. It didn't matter which, it gave them a reason to maintain the fight. That was what counted. That was what got young men to stand up and be counted. The Struggle.

"Do you go back home very often?" Frost asked. It wasn't the safest question, but it was vague enough not to come across as prying, and would hopefully draw Con O'Toole into an actual conversation without him feeling he was being interrogated.

O'Toole leaned forward, speaking in little more than a whisper. "Better if I don't, if you know what I mean. Chances are, me showing up would put an old friend at risk, and you don't do that to old friends."

"An old friend?"

Con looked around the bar. It was doing a steady trade. In the last few minutes, a couple of new punters had come in out of the cold. The barman was occupied with them, towelling down a glass and uncorking a bottle of red wine. No-one else was paying any attention. "Patrick O'Dwyer," Con said, giving Frost a wink.

Jackpot.

"You knew O'Dwyer?" Frost replied, doing his utmost to add a subtle sense of awe to what he said.

O'Toole looked down at his pint, which was well past the half way mark: an obvious hint that the stout and their time together were running out. Frost needed to keep him talking. "Another?" he asked even though he had barely taken a couple of sips from his own pint, his second still untouched.

Con made a show of thinking about it, and then drained his glass. "Why the fuck not, eh? You only live once."

Frost returned from the bar with another pint for the man and a couple of meat and potato pies that ought to keep the inveterate drinker in place long enough to tell his tale. The clock was edging towards twelve.

"You didn't have to do that," O'Toole said, eyeing the pie with more than a little suspicion.

"It's fine, seriously, I can't eat in front of you, and I'm starving, so I'm happy to stand you a pie. It's not like it'll break the bank."

The other man would obviously have preferred an additional pint, but he picked up the knife and fork and made a tentative incision. Steam rose from the centre of the pie, and carried with it the odour of something approaching fresh meat.

Frost waited until the man had taken his first forkful before doing the same.

"So, seriously, you knew Paddy O'Dwyer back in the old country?"

"Of course I did. We grew up together, used to go to the same social, danced with the same girls in the club; bruised a few knuckles and bounced a few heads together, did me and Paddy. And, with a bit of luck, I'll be seeing him again before too long." He took another fork-full of the steaming pie, oblivious to the temperature of the filling.

"You're going back?"

"Don't you listen, lad? I told you, they'd be watching me. I can't go back, coz they've got it in for me and my friends."

"Right, yeah, sorry." Frost knew exactly which kind of people had it in for Con O'Toole. People like him. "Then..." Frost was reluctant to be the one to put the words into his mouth.

The man leaned forward again. "He's already over here, laddy," he whispered conspiratorially.

"You're shitting me," Frost replied, trying hard to hide the fact that this was exactly what he'd been hoping to hear.

"I'm not. I'm deadly shittin' serious, and you know what?"

"What?"

"I'm meeting the old bastard tonight. We're getting together for old time's sake, share a bottle of Bushmills, talk about the old days. Reminisce."

"Sounds like a grand night." It was more than Frost could have hoped for. "You're a very lucky man."

"Lucky?" Con sniffed, then looked at the rapidly diminishing pie. "I guess I am. I mean if I wasn't, I wouldn't be here now eating this fine feast, would I?" He smiled and took another pull on his pint.

Frost didn't push the conversation.

It was time to let the man talk about whatever he wanted to talk about.

Though odds on, the old drunk didn't know what O'Dwyer was over here for. O'Dwyer wasn't dumb. He knew that trusting an alcoholic with his plans would be suicidal.

For the next ten minutes, he listened as the man rambled on with anecdotes about life in Northern Ireland: about the Shankill Road and how the Troubles were in his blood, how he'd run with the Shankill Butchers. Excited at the memory, and putting two and two together he said, "You're not Lenny Murphy's boy, are you?"

Frost knew his history. Lenny Murphy ran the Butchers along with William Marchant and Frankie Currie. Real people, real histories. He wasn't about to lay claim to one of them.

"Nah. Common name, Murphy," he said.

Con nodded.

O'Toole didn't stay at the table long enough for Frost to buy him another pint. Frost was still barely half way down his first, the froth still sticking to the inside of the glass.

"Anyway," O'Toole said. "There are a couple of old pals of mine over there I want to have a sit down with, see if they got a line on the three o'clock at Kilbeggan. Always like a wee flutter on the geegees when I know how the race is going to run, if'n you know what I mean?" He pushed himself up to his feet, giving a slight wobble as the chair grated back on the threadbare carpet.

"I'll be seein' you around, my friend," he said, and offered Frost a drunken handshake.

"Sure thing," said Frost. "I need to be making tracks soon, you know, places to be..."

"Jobs to try not to get. I know the old dole dodge too well. Look after yerself, laddy. Next time, it's on me," O'Toole said giving him an exaggerated wink, then weaved his way across the bar with his near empty glass pointing the way towards a couple of old boys who had obviously been waiting for him to join them.

# TWENTY

The room had no windows.

Air conditioning kept it cool, but there was no way of looking out, no way to see the world out there, or perhaps, more importantly, for the world out there to look in.

"This is Danny," Dawson said, introducing Sir Charles to the man sitting at the computer console. Danny had 'the look'. Fresh from university, already bored with life. Sir Charles was glad: a little boredom ought to make him more pliable, and certainly a disaffected graduate was easier to steer with his helpless old duffer routine than either a woman or a field agent would be. He knew that from bitter experience. He just wasn't good with the ladies. It wasn't that he wasn't charming. He just...bumbled. It didn't matter how many times he rehearsed the lines in his head, or practiced the slight smile in the mirror; a life without female company from school days into the service left him adrift in a sea of hormones. Not even Greta had cured him of that. Now, it was just easier to be asexual, all thoughts of that other life, the possibilities he'd missed out on, dismissed.

Sir Charles held out a hand in greeting.

"Pleased to meet you," he said as the young man accepted it limply.

"Likewise," he said. "Pull up a pew."

Sir Charles wheeled one of the other chairs to sit alongside him, getting a better view of the screen.

"I'll leave you to it then," Dawson turned and walked away without waiting for a response.

"Okay," Danny said, swinging his chair around so that he was closer to the keyboard. "The boss says he wants me to show you how to get logged into the system?"

"Sounds like a good place to start."

He leaned forward to show how intently he was concentrated on what he was being shown.

Danny plucked a post-it note from the edge of the screen and placed it on the patch of desk between them. Sir Charles looked at the piece of yellow paper and read the word, "'Sirchaz1'?"

"That's your user name, hope you don't mind. I needed something to set you up on the system, and that sort of jumped into my head."

"Sir *Chaz*?"

"Yeah, sorry. Like I said, first thing I thought of, and it sounded a bit like a wine."

"It's fine," he said, managing a thin chuckle. "Though I'm more of a cognac man, myself. So I just need to type this in and it gets me into the system?"

"Not so fast," Danny said.

The operator launched into an explanation about needing to set up a password that only he knew and how, once he was in the system, IT would always be able to trace who it was that had logged on, from where, and pick up any anomalous entries should someone try to hack in. He kept the jargon down, which Sir Charles appreciated, and made it sound more James Bond than it really was, which he appreciated, too.

"Tight security," Sir Charles said. "That's good."

Danny's fingers flew over the keyboard, summoning details from the depths of the system.

Sir Charles watched as the screen scrolled, revealing his photograph—the same one that appeared on his ID card—and alongside it, his name, date of birth, address, military record, and personal stuff that he hadn't imagined would be stored somewhere, even in the depths of Whitehall. It was eye-opening.

"Big Brother is watching you," he said.

"Always. And it looks like you've given him plenty to see," he said.

"Ah, it looks more glamorous than it was."

He assumed the dossier would run out of things to say as he scrolled down. After he left the service, he couldn't imagine it was worth maintaining a non-operational journal. His life hadn't been all that exciting to begin with.

"There must be rooms and rooms filled up with this information," he said, thinking of the number of people who worked in the service, and all of the intelligence being collected and collated from the listening post at GCHQ, from undercover operatives and spies. "Is there even a computer large enough to store it all?" He wondered. He'd seen data rooms where there had been banks upon banks of machines back in the '80s, but had no real idea of how much information they were capable of storing. He'd heard something about them being like filing cabinets. That was about as technical as he got.

"They're all networked together," Danny explained. "It's not all on one system. Anyway, here," he handed Sir Charles a white envelope. There was a small chit inside, on it a short-life password that would expire before the end of the day. "Log in with this, then reset the password to something you can remember. Minimum eight characters. If you're smart, you'll include upper- and lower-case letters and a number. Make it memorable, but difficult to guess. So not your pet's name. Not your wife or your favourite football team. Nothing someone who knows you will be able to work out. We don't want anyone watching you, picking up your habits, and getting a back door straight through national security because you decided you had to use your date of birth or national insurance number. Be creative. And I know it's teaching granny to suck eggs, but don't write it down. I'll go grab us coffees while you think about it. Military standard, I presume?"

Sir Charles nodded.

"Great. It's a vending machine, I'm afraid, but it's better than nothing."

"That's fine," Sir Charles replied, not taking his eyes off the screen, watching as the cursor blinked in the box.

His fingers hovered over the keyboard while he thought for a moment.

Eventually he typed, '19Prague68' with each key producing an asterix in the box before he was asked to enter the same password again to make sure the machine had it correct.

"All done?" Danny asked, returning with a couple of plastic cups with a steaming liquid that couldn't have been called coffee under the Trades Descriptions Act. Sir Charles didn't touch his.

"I think so," he said as the man tapped a couple of keys to confirm that he was inside the system.

"Excellent. Now what are you looking for, exactly?"

"The latest intelligence on Patrick O'Dwyer, for a start. And a list of anyone he might have direct contact with in London, plus known associates, particularly anyone who might have entered the country or been released from prison in the last three months."

"That's going to take a while, I'm afraid."

"How come?"

"Our machines are all connected, but they're not connected to everyone else's, if that makes sense? I can put in a request to GCHQ. They'll trawl their logs for phone intercepts, that kind of thing. The prison service is a different matter altogether. The police are unlikely to have alerted us of anything unless they had real suspicions that something was going on. It's not an exact science: too many variables. But we'll get there. We just need to refine the search parameters a bit. Start with the known associates, cross-reference border controls; that kind of thing."

"What about O'Dwyer himself, then?" Sir Charles's worse fears were coming true. All the agencies would be territorial. It was in their nature to hoard knowledge. He watched as the man called up O'Dwyer's file on the screen, only to find that access was denied.

"What's the problem?" Sir Charles asked as the man input the request again.

"It would seem that your security clearance isn't high enough," Danny said.

"That's ridiculous."

"No, it's fine. We just need to get your access upgraded on this thing. I'll send a request in. We should be able to get it sorted before too long."

"How long are we talking about? An hour? I suppose I could grab some lunch and return."

The younger man laughed. "With a little luck and a following wind we *might* have the authorisation in place for you to have access tomorrow."

"Tomorrow? Not good enough. There must be something you can do. A call you can make to chivvy things along?"

Danny tried something different.

This time, the computer responded by scrolling up a list of sightings: times, dates and locations. Sir Charles looked at the screen. There was nothing on it that he hadn't seen before. He said as much.

"It's all I can get, I'm afraid."

Sir Charles sat for a moment. "This is it? This is all I can get?"

"Until we get your clearance sorted out. Sorry."

It didn't really matter what was on the screen now; he had already got what he had come for. A legitimate way into the system for Philip.

"Can I leave it with you to try to get my clearance sorted, or do I need to speak to someone?"

"It's fine. I'll get it sorted for you. But best if we log you out of this before you disappear." He used the mouse to clear the details that were on the screen before the log in page returned again. "Done."

"And I'll be able to log into the network from outside? Or will I need to come back in?"

"Technically, you can open a pipe. I'll give you a program to put on your home system, but it'll be a lot easier for you to just log in from here. I know it's a drag coming into the offices, but that way I get to help you, too, so it'll save time."

"That's very decent of you."

"No problem. Let me grab you a floppy and put the access routine on it. I'll write the address you need on the disk. It's all fairly self-explanatory."

"Again, my thanks, Danny. You've been very helpful."

# TWENTY ONE

His phone bleeped the moment he stepped outside the building.

He assumed that meant that the fabric of the building was shielded from invasive signals by design. One thing the service were good at was foresight; the possibility of a mobile phone signal penetrating into the heart of MI5 might be the stuff of James Bond, but as he was rapidly learning, the world was changing fast, every technological leap a giant one that outstripped everything thought possible only a few short years before. He played back the message. It was Henry from his club.

"Sir Charles. I have been asked to relay a message to you, but the young man who left it was adamant I should only give it to you in person. If you would care to call me back when it's convenient."

Sir Charles punched the button to return the call, glad that the other man had not left any details on the phone. Again, he had no idea if his calls were being listened to, or his voice mailbox monitored, but it was best not to take unnecessary risks.

The ring signal cycled twice before Henry's unflappable voice—always calm, always reliable—said, "Sir Charles, thank you for calling back so quickly."

"You have word from Mr. Frost for me?"

"Yes, sir. Let me read it back to you," there was the sound of ruffling pages. "There's a gentleman by the name of Connor O'Toole, a regular at a public house in Holborn: Malone's. He's meeting the target tonight. Your man doesn't know where, but says the target is definitely in the city." There was a moment's pause as he closed the book. "I hope that makes sense to you, sir? I read it back to him for confirmation, but he was in a call box and the traffic was a little noisy so I can't be sure I got it exactly correct."

"You did well, Henry. It makes perfect sense. Thank you."

"Pleasure, Sir," the man said, and then hung up.

So Frost had come good.

He hadn't been sure he would when he'd met him in that hospital room. Frost was a good guy. He understood the cost. He knew that being on the side of the angels sometimes required immense sacrifice. That was why he pulled the trigger and put bullets into Jimmy Shannon's corpse without already knowing he was dead. Frost was committed to completing the story. And that was what he'd signed up to do.

Sir Charles stood on the steps, contemplating turning around and going back into the secure facility to see what information they held on Connor O'Toole; but he was old school. Why use a computer when you can do the business voice-to-voice, if not face-to-face? It was certainly quicker for a man with his computer skills to make a phone call.

He couldn't help it; he was beginning to enjoy himself. There was an adrenal buzz to this job, knowing the stakes, knowing he was the difference. It felt good to be challenged again. This, as much as he was loath to admit it, was what he lived for.

"Philip," he said when his first call connected.

Terry was already heading towards him, though the traffic was slow-moving.

Sir Charles raised a hand to acknowledge him as he approached.

"Charley."

"Have you had your morning delivery?"

"I certainly have. I'm impressed, boss. Crack of dawn, they were here with everything."

"Like I said, a title opens doors. How long will it take you to get everything up and running?"

"Already done. It's loading the software patches now."

"Excellent. Do you have a pen and paper handy?"

"Just a sec," he said.

Sir Charles could hear him scrambling around for something to write on, the hacker's breathing loud in his air.

"Shoot," he said eventually.

"User name SirChaz1," he spelled out, emphasising the capital S, capital C, in case it was important. "Password 19Prague68."

"Is this what I think it is?"

"Assuming you think it's your—"

"Don't say it—not an insecure line. You don't know who's listening. Is there a TELNET address or something on it? God... you wouldn't have a clue, would you? It could be Sanskrit."

"Actually, I read Sanskrit fluently. There are numbers punctuated by full stops written on the label of the floppy disk. Do you need them?"

"No. I know what I'm doing. I'll be fine without the handshake."

"You do realise how much I'm trusting you?"

"Of course I do."

"Good. Now, I know you're going to be struggling with temptation, and this makes me a little like the serpent with the apple, taunting you to take a bite. Don't. No matter how much you want to go in and poke around, don't. Not until we *need* to. I don't want to be pulled in off the streets because they think my account has been compromised. Understood?"

"You have my word. So, did you get to play around while you were inside?"

"Not particularly. My security clearance wasn't high enough to get at everything I wanted to see. They've promised to review it, but that could take days given the hell that is the bureaucracy of Her Majesty's chosen ones."

"Shouldn't be an issue. I can probably raise it myself."

"Better if you don't, if possible. It's likely to set all kinds of alarm bells ringing."

"You're the boss. How come they didn't set it up high enough in the first place?"

"That, my young friend, is a very good question. But it certainly made sure that I couldn't look at something I wanted to from back in the day."

"So they're hiding something from you?"

"Or trying to draw me in."

"Okay, boss, where do you want me to start?"

"Anything you can find on Patrick O'Dwyer and any known associates. I need to know if any of them own or rent a property in the Greater London area, or have booked into a hotel in the last week or so."

"Isn't that where MI5 would have started before they called you in?"

"You would think so, wouldn't you? They seemed to be trying to tell me that their system wasn't set up to do that kind of thing, which seems suspect. How long do you think it's going to take you?"

"Hard to say. I should be getting the first results back from the crawler within the hour, but to be honest, it'll probably take a couple more to get anything meaningful. I'm only going to be able to get into the main hotel chains. If they've booked into a small, private hotel, or a B&B, there's no guarantee there will even be a computer footprint. Some people still think it's 1984."

Sir Charles wasn't entirely sure if that was a literary reference or a technological one, but it worked on both levels. "I understand. Get me what you can. I'll check in later. You might not hear from me for a few hours; I've got something to take care of." He hung up. Now that he'd said it aloud, he was sure that something hadn't been one hundred percent right about his visit inside the building. They hadn't put up barriers, security screens or anything physical to stop him getting in, at least not in a practical sense, but they were definitely making it difficult to get anything beyond the basic info he already had.

Was he being paranoid, or was he missing something?

Terry had been waiting patiently at the side of the road while he completed the call.

"Everything all right, sir?" he asked. "That didn't take as long as I expected."

"I'm a fast learner," he said with a smile.

"So where to now?"

"I need to find a pub called Malone's," he began.

"In Holborn?"

"That's the one. Do you know it?"

"I've been in a couple of times. It's an Irish pub, live music most nights, not exactly got the best reputation. Bit rough."

"I don't suppose you know a man called Connor O'Toole? Con?"

"Sorry," his driver shook his head. "Doesn't ring any bells. Is he holding our smoking gun?"

"Well, let's just say he's a person of interest right now."

"This come from your man on the inside?"

"He's not mine."

"But you're sure you can trust him?"

"I'm not really sure who I can trust at the moment, Terry."

"Healthy distrust never hurt anyone."

"Indeed."

"So what's the plan, hit the pub, bring in O'Toole?"

"No. We use him. Go in there all guns blazing, we'll end up with another body to scrape up of the road. We watch him and hope he leads us to O'Dwyer. Frost seems to think that they are meeting tonight."

"Want me to put a surveillance team on O'Toole?"

"Better we do it ourselves, I think, given the heavy-handed inference from your paymasters that this was to be low key."

"Strikes me it's a bit of a waste of your time, though. Want me to do it?"

"You?"

"Why not? It's a pub. I'm going to stand out a lot less than you, no offense."

Sir Charles nodded. "Drop me somewhere I'm likely to be able to get a cab. I'll make my own way to Philip's place."

"Sir. And you're sure you don't want me to pick him up? I could take him somewhere. Do it nice and quiet. No-one would know."

Sir Charles didn't doubt it for a moment.

He even indulged the possibility of interrogating the man, breaking him. But no: his first instinct was the right one.

Watch O'Toole, and hope that he would lead them to O'Dwyer. Patience could be the greatest of weapons. O'Toole might crack under interrogation and sell out O'Dwyer, but there was always the risk he'd be missed. And if he didn't know where O'Dwyer was, they would have shot their load for nothing.

"I'm sure. Locate him, observe; do not engage. And if, for a moment, you suspect you've been made, disengage. We don't want O'Dwyer going to ground."

"Understood," Terry said.

# TWENTY TWO

The taxi driver had been reluctant to take Sir Charles to Philip's estate without being paid cash up front.

"You sure that this is *really* where you want to go, guv?"

"I'm sure," he said, settling back into the seat. The taxi smelled of vomit from the night before. It wasn't the most pleasant 'London Experience'. Certainly not one for the Tourist Board to put in their brochures.

The traffic moved smoothly, but with no great haste. It gave him time to think, and that was a precious commodity.

The driver wanted to talk, as most of his kind seemed to, filling the silence of their day with constant blather, most of it racist or homophobic or just misinformed, unless the topic was football. Sir Charles hoped that his terse responses would be enough to deter him.

Something nagged away at the back of his brain.

He was probably seeing a mystery or a conspiracy where there was none, but why would the Secret Service call him into an operation, and then withhold information from him? That didn't make sense.

The answer was going to be either cock-up or cover-up; this had to be cock-up.

No-one had thought to pass on his clearance status to the junior who set his security level on the computer system: just an oversight, no more than that. It happened all the time when everything needed to be filled out in triplicate. But it was like trying to do the job with one hand tied behind his back.

The good news was that his free hand was Philip, and he wasn't bound by the same restrictions and protocols that an MI5 operative would have been, so all wasn't lost.

He watched the buildings go by, from redbrick to Victorian terrace, to Edwardian and back to redbrick as the car made slow but steady progress. The driver leaned on his horn when anything on two wheels cut across him, stealing the road. Sir Charles ignored the curses. Another horn sounded as a courier cut across first one lane of traffic and then another, then ran a red light on his bike.

The whole place seemed to close in on him, the traffic crowding out his thoughts.

After half a lifetime of service on the frontline, he'd grown used to the peace and quiet of his family home. The tranquillity of Nonesuch couldn't have been more different to the living hell of London.

He glanced out of the window again.

The traffic was moving much more freely as they drove through a bleak part of town, where the front gardens of half the houses had been turned into dumping grounds for old television sets, prams and broken toys. In the distance, he saw the high rise of a cluster of tower blocks. He couldn't imagine living like that.

They drove past the restaurant where they had eaten the night before, and after negotiating a sequence of streets where overflowing garbage bins spilled their contents onto the pavement, came to a halt alongside a car that looked as if it was held together by the rust eating into its bodywork. The accumulation of dirt on the windscreen along with the flat front tyre was a good indication it hadn't moved for some time.

Sir Charles gave the driver a healthy tip, even though he had already been paid for the ride.

"You're not going to find it easy to get a cab from here, guv. It's not the kind of place we like to come," the driver said as he handed him a business card. "Give this number a call when you're ready and tell them that Derek gave you the card. They'll get a message to me and I'll pick you up, as long as I'm not out on the other side of town."

"Very kind of you," Sir Charles said, hoping he wouldn't need to make the call. It all depended on what happened with Terry and O'Toole.

It took a couple of minutes to find the right building from the huddled blocks of flats, each in the shadow of the next. He understood why Philip had been happy to meet him at the restaurant rather than bring him here. The reek of piss was oppressive, but nowhere nearly as bad as the sour stench of despair. There was no ventilation on the concrete stairway, despite the broken windows on every landing. Three youths clustered around a ghetto blaster on the next landing, seemingly oblivious to the smell.

They gave him a sly glance as he climbed past them, but their only move was to hide something out of his sight.

He didn't need to see what they were hiding to know what it was.

He could smell the too-sweet smoke. Even the piss couldn't mask it.

He carried on climbing, until eventually he stood outside a door with white peeling paint and a doorbell that didn't ring.

He rapped his knuckles on a pane of poorly-fitted glass set into the doorframe, careful not to knock too hard for fear it would fall out. A moment later, he heard the sounds of movement coming towards him.

Philip opened the door.

The hacker turned his back on him and headed back inside without so much as a hello.

"Everything all right?" Sir Charles called after the retreating figure.

"Yeah, fine," he replied, leading the way into a room that seemed to be full to bursting with electronic equipment.

"You sure? You don't sound fine."

"I'd forgotten that today would have been my day to have my son. His mother is going ballistic. She says I'm not 'reliable' and that I don't care."

"I'm sure that's not true, and I'm sorry if I've caused you problems. I confess I didn't even know that you had a son."

"Neither did I, until I got out. We broke up before I got sent down. Didn't even know that she was pregnant."

"Would you like me to have a word with her? Maybe I can explain?" He didn't know exactly what he could explain, but he made the offer anyway. He looked at the young hacker. He didn't see an ex-con, he saw a young man who needed a chance to show what he was capable of doing.

"I doubt it will make any difference," Philip said. "She's been looking for an excuse stop me spending time with him."

"Well, when this is all over..."

"It won't make any difference." He slumped into the room's only chair and started hammering on the keys of the keyboard in front of him. A string of characters began to appear on the screen. It meant nothing to Sir Charles, but why would it?

Latin would have meant nothing to his companion, and that's basically what it was: a different language.

Changing the subject was probably a smart move, but the photograph on the wall of a small boy, no more than a couple of years old at the time it was taken, kept smiling at him from above the two computer screens.

"Have you managed to get anything yet?"

"Some," he said, handing over a sheaf of paper. "These are the names and addresses of the people who came up as known associates."

"Any trouble getting them?" he said riffling through the pages.

"Not really. This stuff isn't hard to find if you know where to look. I thought I'd been rumbled a couple of times, but managed to shut down before anyone could trace it back to me."

"MI5?"

"Not yet. I resisted temptation, just like you asked. The apple may be tempting, but there was plenty of other low-hanging fruit. I've got all this data ready to pump back into the MI5 files to see how many matches we come up with there. Just give me the word."

Sir Charles took the floppy disk from his pocket and handed it over to the hacker. "Hopefully this will help."

"Should do."

He flicked through the stack of papers again.

There was too much information, that much was obvious. They'd cast the net too wide. It needed to be narrowed down. Chances were, the most up-to-date information would be in the counter-terrorism files of MI5.

"Let's give it a whirl, then," he said. "There's no point in hanging around."

Philip adjusted his chair, and then flexed the fingers of each hand. Sir Charles winced when he heard the young man's knuckles crack. His fingers seemed to be little more than a blur as they hit the keys without him taking his eyes away from one of the screens. Sir Charles could not help but admire the other man's skill. With barely a pause, Philip lifted one hand from the keyboard and picked up the mug that sat on the desk beside him, holding it out for Sir Charles to take from him. He didn't need to be asked to fill it.

"Coffee?"

"Black. Three sugars," he replied. The screen lit up his face. His fingers were motionless for a moment, poised above the keys. Sir Charles headed through to the small kitchen and left him to it. It looked as if it hadn't been cleaned for a least a month. Every piece of crockery he owned was piled up in the sink unwashed. He rinsed out the mug and set the kettle to boil. He wasn't about to risk listeria himself. By the time he returned, Philip was leaning back in the chair with his hands clasped behind his head, looking very satisfied with himself.

"How is it going?"

"I'm in. I might not have managed to do it without your disk, though. Clever stuff. But the minute this bit of code has uploaded, I'll be logging out. We don't need to be in there longer than it takes to ask the question."

"What about the answer?"

"It's going to be emailed to me."

"Won't that make it easy to trace?"

"Only if they want to try to chase it through half a dozen countries and twice as many anonymisers."

The other PC pinged an alert.

Philip turned his attention to the second screen and opened up the email that had arrived. Philip accepted the coffee without looking away from the screen. He opened the file attached to the email. Sir Charles tried to read over his shoulder, but the lines were scrolling by too quickly to read. Maybe Philip knew what he was looking for. Eventually he reached the end, and the last entry was still long enough for him to read it.

"What's that?" Sir Charles asked, his heart suddenly beating faster than it had any right to. He stared at the name on the screen, filled with a mixture of confusion, fear and excitement. There was an address, too, but he wasn't looking at it. The name had his complete attention. Greta Ciurak.

"That? Nothing. That's a mistake."

It wasn't. It couldn't be. "What do you mean, a mistake?"

"When I was putting in the search details I added a couple of extra fields of information that weren't needed."

"Like what?"

"You. I figured that there was a reason why you'd been asked to look into this. I don't believe in coincidences where the Government are concerned. I figured I'd see if putting you into the mix narrowed down the search at all."

"The other field? You said there were a couple."

"Your password. What can I say? 19Prague68 is pretty specific. Couldn't help but wonder why you'd chosen it. There had to be some significance. You know how the mind works. It's all about unconscious connections. This woman here, Greta Ciurak, connects you and Patrick O'Dwyer, has an address in London, and is linked to Prague in 1968. She fulfills all four parameters."

"That's impossible."

"Are you sure?"

"Of course I'm sure."

"It doesn't make sense."

"Well, what you're looking at here is an address that MI5 have on file for her. It's current. Sorry if I overstepped the mark. But she's the only intersection. Is there a problem?"

"You could say that. I was under the impression she died in 1968."

# TWENTY THREE

Ronan Frost waited in his flat.

He hated waiting.

He really hated waiting.

Especially when he knew something was about to kick off.

He wanted to be easy to track down, in case they came looking for him.

They'd have found him in Malone's, he was sure, but this was easier. Private.

There was a car in the parking bays on the forecourt that didn't belong there.

He had done everything he could to make sure that he wasn't followed when he left the pub in search of a phone box, but he wasn't an idiot. He knew Five would be watching him. He couldn't let himself worry about it, so he let them get on with doing their thing, knowing they had his back if things went tits-up.

The building shifted from the near silence of the early afternoon to the deafening cauldron of children coming home from school. The sky was already starting to fall dark. A few streetlights—those that weren't shattered—began to glow in the gloom. Doors slammed. The shouting began all over again, arguments picked up as if there'd been no break since the morning. Life on the estate: an endless merry-go-round that never really stopped.

He caught sight of the shape on the other side of the door just before it opened. No knock, again. Only one man came and went without knocking.

"Still not tidied up, then? The youth of today. Disgusting."

"Well, you know how it is, Lorcan. One thing after another and all that, not enough hours in the day."

Lorcan Kelly looked around disapprovingly, but refrained from further comment. This wasn't the way that Frost chose to live, but it suited Liam Murphy; that was what mattered. It was important to sell the legend. Anything else would have been wrong. The world wasn't filled with fastidious rebels. He was supposed to be a young man, away from home for the first time, looking to stand on his own two feet. A bit out of his depth. Vulnerable. The perfect recruit for the Republican cause.

"Time to go," Kelly said.

"Right now?"

"Right now. Or have you got somewhere else you need to be, soft lad? Maybe heading back to the pub?"

"The pub?" His palms felt greasy as he realised that his fears about having been watched were well founded. Maybe it wasn't Five who had his back, but the cell who were out to get it?

"Con told me that you were a bit flash with the cash, plying him with beer. You're a very generous man."

"I bought him a pie and a couple of pints. He's an interesting bloke."

"He's a fucking drunk with a big gob is what he is. Now, let's move it."

Frost looked around. This was it. Whatever was going to happen was going to happen tonight. There was every chance

**143**

he'd never set foot in this shithole again. He was already dreaming of taking himself off to the sun somewhere, to soak up some rays and try and learn how to be himself again, as he walked out of the door.

The transit van had been reversed close to the exit at the bottom of the stairwell. Frost didn't recognise the man who opened the doors as they approached. He was thickset, no neck, well over six feet tall and carrying enough muscle to suggest he was one of the many navvies the old country supplied to the city's building sites. Frost was handy with his fists. He could take most people in a fair fight, and just about anyone in an unfair one, but he didn't fancy his chances against a man mountain like this in a confined space. Frost only caught a glimpse of the dark shape huddled in one of the far corners before he felt a sharp shove in the back that sent him stumbling forwards. He reached out to brace himself instinctively as the big guy bundled him inside.

A moment later the doors were slammed behind him and he was plunged into darkness.

Frost clenched his teeth, still on hands and knees, as the van peeled away from the estate. He resisted the temptation to call out, to hammer on the door or the panelled walls, demanding to know what the hell was going on. He knew what was going on. He was up to his neck in faecal matter and needed to stay calm, or it was going to get very fucking messy.

They knew they had a traitor in their midst.

"I should never have talked to you, you sack of shit," a voice said in the darkness.

"Con?"

"Don't even mention my name, you dirty bastard. You dirty fucking bastard," though he pronounced it bas-tid. "I should never have spoken to you. They won't believe that I

**144**

didn't tell you anything. They just said that I shouldn't have been talking to you. I shouldn't have trusted you coz you're bent. I'm fucked because of you, you fucker."

"I don't know what you're talking about, Con. I'm not bent. I haven't told anyone we've talked, only Lorcan, said I stood you a couple of beers," Frost lied, the words tripping easily from his lips. "I would never say anything. Jesus, Con, what do you take me for?"

"Try telling them that," the old man said in the darkness. The van slowed, turned, the movement pushing them up against the side, and then accelerated away again, out of the estate. Frost could only hope the watchers were Five, and that they were on top of their game, or he was fucked. They'd have orders to let shit play out, not interfere until they had absolutely no alternative. He could live with that.

He just had to sit tight.

He managed to fight against the lurch of the vehicle and clamber into a seated position, his back up against the panelled wall. The metal vibrated against his spine. He felt every heave and bump as the wheels hit the potholes in the road.

"Where are they taking us?" Frost asked.

"Jesus Fuck lad, are you simple? To see Paddy, of course. Now that you know he's here, they are going to have to keep you out of the way until what's done is done. It's that or..."

"Or what?"

"Maybe it'd just be easier if you took a long journey and didn't come back."

# TWENTY FOUR

Sir Charles was still looking at the name and address on the screen when his phone rang.

Terry.

"Anything to report?"

"Got here too late, boss. A red transit van took off just as I arrived. By the sounds of it, our man was bundled into the back. Missed him by a minute, no more. Sorry."

"Can't be helped," he replied, more than a little frustrated that the only lead that Frost had been able to give them had slipped through their fingers so easily.

"I managed to find out where he lives, so I headed there just in case. No sign of him or the van."

"Pick me up at Philip's place. We may have found something."

"On my way. Hope whatever you've found makes up for this."

"So do I," Sir Charles said.

But how could she be alive, he wondered? Here, in London, and not have reached out to him? The Service knew she was here, and they'd deliberately kept it from him. That was the answer to the riddle of his downgraded security clearance.

Now he had a phone number to go with the address.

He could call her, but what would he say? Would she want to hear from him? He was a ghost from the past, and as much as he'd loved her once upon a time, it had been one-way traffic. She hadn't even known he'd carried a torch for her. She'd only had eyes for Paddy.

But the more he thought about it, the more obvious it became that if she was alive, she could well be the missing link that'd take him to Paddy O'Dwyer. A fool in love, and all of that.

"Can you tell how long she's lived at this address?" he asked.

"That ought to be a lot easier to find out," Philip said, attacking the keyboard again. "The Land Registry doesn't seem to think they have anything to hide. Same goes for the Electoral Register. Give me a sec."

He was right. It took a matter of minutes to get into both, and even less time to discover that Greta had owned the house for more than twenty years, yet did not appear on the register of voters.

"Strange," Philip said.

"Not really. Remember, she's Czech; nothing to say she's been made a British citizen."

"And yet she's been able to live here all this time?"

"Let's say that the British Government owe her a lot."

"Want me to print everything out?" he asked.

"I don't think that will be necessary," Sir Charles said.

He scribbled the address down on a piece of paper and tucked it inside his jacket pocket.

"Anything else you need me to do?"

"Can you keep your phone line free?"

"Sure. I had a second line installed just to be able to use the phone and stay on line. Makes life much simpler."

Sir Charles knew that his expression probably made him look more than a little vacant. He could tap a phone, he could divert calls to another number, he could even shin up an old-style telegraph pole and tap into the exchange, but it wasn't just a case of technology starting to leave him behind: it was rapidly approaching a different millennium to the one he was living in. He'd made the decision to let it go a few years back. Maybe that had been a mistake. He'd never expected to wind up back in this line of work, though.

"Stay here. I'll call you if I need you."

He headed down stairs to wait for Terry.

He wanted to make a call to Dawson to see if there'd been a Sit Rep from Frost, and thought it best not to make it from Philip's apartment, in case they were monitoring his cell signal or something that would ping an alert somewhere deep in the heart of some MoD dungeon. He didn't want them to set loose the dogs of war on poor old Philip.

It wasn't until he stepped outside again that he realised just how loud the hum of equipment really was.

One thing he'd learned a long time ago was that the easiest way to avoid answering questions is to avoid being asked them in the first place. That was one of those lessons that had been ingrained in him to the point of becoming second nature. The problem was that all of those ducked and dodged questions were now beginning to work their way back around to him.

He didn't have to wait long to be connected.

"Sir Charles. I'm so glad that you've called, you were on a long list of people I needed to get hold of today."

On a long list.

Meaning not important enough to get individual treatment.

He was being played here.

He knew it.

It was all beginning to crystallise in his mind—why him? Why drag him out of retirement to front this so-called task force?

He had an answer.

He didn't like the answer, but that didn't mean it was wrong. Far from it. It almost certainly guaranteed it was right.

"Oh? Why were you going to try to get hold of me? Problem?" He was fishing. Did they know already that Philip had accessed the system remotely using his credentials? No. He'd be able to hear the sirens if they'd worked that out.

"Nothing urgent. Just wanted to apologise that your security clearance was wrong. We've taken care of it now. If you want to come in again I can make sure that Danny's around to help you out?"

"Actually, I don't think I'm going to need it," he said.

"Really?"

"Yes. Some good old fashioned leg work has turned up a lead that might just pan out."

"Excellent. That's exactly why we wanted you in on this. Care to share?"

*Absolutely not*, he thought. Not that he could actually say that. It was down to trust again, and one person he was fairly sure he didn't trust was Michael Dawson. "It's a long shot. It'll probably come to nothing, but I'll let you know if anything develops." He certainly wasn't going to let on that he knew Greta was in London. She was a piece in the puzzle they could easily have put into place. The only reason they wouldn't have told him she was alive was if they intended to dangle him out there like a worm on a hook to reel Paddy in. "Any news on Frost?" he asked, changing the subject. They didn't need to know this particular worm had turned, for a little while, yet.

"Nothing at all."

"But you've still got eyes on him?"

"Of course. There's been nothing from them."

"And you've checked in with them?"

"There's a changeover due in an hour. We'll get a Situation Report from the men on the ground then."

"I don't like it. Try and raise them now."

"There's really no need."

"Humour me."

"Okay, hold on a minute." Dawson shouted something across the room, but the hand he'd placed over the mouthpiece muffled the words. A couple of seconds later he came back on the line. "They're not responding."

"What's the address?"

"He's on the Rothery Estate, Twenty-Seven Hogarth Court. One of the high rises."

"That's on the way that I'm heading. I'll take a look."

"I don't know—"

"Look, like it or not, we're dealing with terrorists no matter what flag they are fighting under. You brought me in because you think that I'm a better man for this particular job that anyone you currently have on the payroll, and right now my instinct is that your man's in trouble. It's your choice; are you going to hang him out to dry?"

"Of course not."

"That's the right answer. Keep trying to raise the agents you've got out in the field. I'll be there soon enough. What car am I looking for?"

"It's an unmarked Escort. Racing green."

"Roger that. Don't worry; I know what I'm doing. I won't blow their cover."

*It might already be too late for that*, Sir Charles thought.

# TWENTY FIVE

Eventually, the van came to a halt.

Frost had tried to keep count of the number of turns they'd taken, but after a couple of minutes it had become just about impossible to keep up with the count, so instead, he'd focused on trying to identify sounds, anything unique that might give him a clue as to where they were being taken. A couple of times, he had heard the distinctive rumble and the screech of brakes from an Underground train on a stretch of track where it was travelling above ground. They'd driven to somewhere on the outskirts of Greater London. He didn't think they'd crossed the river, so that meant north, but that didn't narrow it down much—until he heard the roar of an airplane somewhere above them. That certainly narrowed things down. He went through the options: Luton and Stansted, London City Airport. That was north and central. Docklands.

The giveaway sound was the sonic boom.

They were on the Concord's flight path, that changed the options.

When the doors opened, Frost blinked against the glare of a streetlight that pierced the darkness.

He checked on Con. The old drunk didn't have any obvious bruises to suggest he'd been worked over before they threw him in the back of the van.

"Move it, the pair of you," the weasel said, one hand still on one of the doors.

Frost allowed the old man to clamber out first, then followed him. It felt good to be out into the fresh air again, all things considered. Better than being cooped up in the back of the van, at least. He managed a glance up and down the road, but there was nothing to see. No further clues as to where they were.

One side of the road was an endless row of terraced houses with the smallest squares of front garden. On the other side of the road, industrial buildings. *Which answers the question why the chicken crossed,* he thought.

"Inside," the man said. "Someone wants to meet you."

It was firm, but if they thought he was the rat, they weren't being overly threatening. Maybe just because they didn't need to. Less is more.

Frost said nothing. He followed the old drunk into the house.

A steep staircase lay a little way ahead of them, leading up into darkness. The curtains were drawn up there, blocking the light out. They were ushered past the door that led to the front room, where a woman sat watching television in the dark. Frost caught a glimpse of her face as the screen cast shadows over it, turning her vaguely monstrous. Another door off the passage led into a back room. The dining table had been turned into a work surface. It didn't take Frost more than a glance to know that there was enough material there to make half a dozen bombs. He tried not to let his expression change. This was it: the beating heart of the cell.

"Quite something, isn't it?" the man sitting at the table said, putting down the pair of pliers he had been holding when they walked in.

"It certainly is," Frost replied.

"Good to see you again, Paddy," Con said, making his way around the table to give the man a hug as he got to his feet. So this was the man Five were so eager to get their hands on. Looking at the paraphernalia on the table, it was obvious why. "This eejit here thinks you're gonna take them pliers to his knackers and twist 'em off." He chuckled at that.

"You boys been having some fun at his expense, have you?" Paddy O'Dwyer said, shaking his head.

"Gotta test his loyalty, make sure he's one of us," Lorcan Kelly said.

"And you thought Con here was the man to do it?" Paddy smiled. "You bunch of bastards." He turned to Frost. "So, you must be the infamous Liam Murphy?" He held out a hand in welcome. "I've heard a *lot* about you, lad."

"Good stuff, I hope," Frost said, feeling Paddy's calluses against his palm.

"Mostly," he said with a wry smile.

"So what do you want me to do? I'll be honest, I don't know shit about bombs," Frost said.

"No worries, son. That's why they've asked me to come over here. This is my particular area of expertise, hard earned from the good men and women of Her Majesty's Armed Forces. I paid attention in school." Again, that smile. "Figured I'd take the opportunity to look up a couple of old friends while I'm here."

"Mixing business with pleasure, eh?" Frost let out a nervous laughed, and hoped that it was convincing enough.

"You could say that. Now, once I've finished putting these together, we can share a bottle of the good stuff and toast the beginning of a beautiful friendship."

"Which is better than getting my balls sliced off," Frost said.

"Certainly is. The only thing you need to worry about is driving. You can do that, right?" Frost nodded. "Good. I want you to drive me and these little beauties into the City so we can put them in place. Big day tomorrow. We need everything ready to go. No mistakes. We're gonna shake the world, my friend. This time tomorrow, everyone will know who we are."

"I'm not entirely sure that's a good thing," Frost said with a smile of his own. He was trying to remember anything he'd heard about events coming up in the City, but he couldn't think of anything remotely visible, or with a high enough profile to warrant an IRA attack.

"You look a little confused, son. In fact, I'm guessing you're trying to think what the feck is happening the morrow, and you can't think of anything, can you? See, not everything makes it into the papers. Tomorrow's all hush-hush. Big meeting. But they're smart, these politicos. Cheap fuckers, too. If no-one knows about it, they don't have to worry about security so much, see?"

Frost had been out of the loop for so long he couldn't even be sure who would be responsible for a visiting dignitary's security. Maybe they'd bring their own men? Pick up a detail from MI5? The SAS? There had to be a leak somewhere though; someone connected to O'Dwyer, which hinted at Five rather than the PM's office.

"We even know what kind of security there will be," O'Dwyer said, enjoying the look of surprise on Frost's face.

"Jesus, that opens up a world of possibilities," Frost breathed.

"You're not wrong there. All we need to do is make sure that we take advantage of the situation."

Frost wanted to push the man, ask him questions about the target, but it was way too soon for that.

"Hey, man—well, anything you need me to do," he said. "You know…"

"I know, son. We're writing our names in history, right up with Guy Fawkes. You'll be there with us. You've got the right stuff."

# TWENTY SIX

It wasn't hard for Sir Charles to pick out the racing green Ford Escort amongst the battered and rusted wrecks that were half-parked, half-abandoned in the car park close to the block of flats in the heart of the Rothery Estate. A couple of the cars were standing on bricks, their wheels long since removed, their paintwork scarred with graffiti, going nowhere. Could they even be called cars anymore, he wondered, if they've been robbed of their primary purpose?

"Park over there," Sir Charles said, pointing to a space reserved for emergency vehicles. "I'll walk around the building. Don't want to blow their cover, assuming they haven't been spotted already."

He got a few glances from a gaggle of kids kicking a football against the far side of the building. They grabbed their ball, as he grew closer, ready to run away. Sadly, he realised, their first instinct was to look at the old man walking towards them and think: pervert. He kept on walking, not wanting to risk the wrath of some tattooed dad looking for trouble. Less than a minute later he could hear the steady *thud, thud, thud,* of the ball thumping against the wall again.

As he approached the car from behind, he could make out the shape of two heads in the front seats, even though the Escort was parked up well away from the single working streetlight in the neighbourhood. There was no glow from the dashboard.

He walked past the car toward the stairwell, giving the briefest of glances inside.

There was no movement.

They hadn't so much as registered his presence.

Sloppy.

Once he reached the stairwell, he paused, then doubled back to the car, confident that there was no-one else watching.

Sir Charles leaned down and tapped on the window.

Nothing.

He crouched down and peered in through the glass.

Then opened the door.

He had smelt death before.

It had a unique repugnance.

He recognised it the instant air escaped from the car.

Gunshot wounds to the head and chest. Dark stains. No signs of life. He reached in to check the nearest man's carotid artery. Dead. His skin was already cold to the touch.

Two men, Service operatives, taken out in their car in broad daylight? In London? Sure, the Rothery was a wart on the genitalia of the city, but even in a hellhole like this, gunshots should have been reported. Yet people were frightened; they hid behind closed doors, afraid to raise their heads above the parapet in case they took a bullet themselves. The Rothery was the kind of place where violence was a legitimate currency.

Sir Charles closed the door and wiped his prints from the handle.

He'd have to get Terry to call it in, and hope a cleanup team made it to the scene before the police stumbled onto the vehicle and the whole mess escalated. He looked across the way at the kids playing wall ball. They didn't need to see this.

What did this mean for Frost?

Nothing good.

Yes, conceivably, whoever had killed these two could have assumed they were just an MI5 surveillance team, keeping an eye on Frost because they had recognised him from the hospital murder, and hoped to follow him up the chain to someone else in the cell. Or they could have made him. Fifty-fifty. Whichever way the odds tumbled, he couldn't leave Frost hanging out to dry.

The lift wasn't working.

He took the stairs two at a time, remembering a time when he had been running away from instead of towards danger, in a place not so different to this.

His feet echoed on the concrete steps, just as they had on cobbled streets back then.

He felt undressed and unprepared going into action without a gun, especially with evidence that the other team were playing for keeps.

Protocol was to wait for backup, but the one thing Frost didn't have if he was in trouble was time.

Terry would be carrying.

Running up the stairs, he called through to the man, summoning him up to Frost's place on the eleventh floor.

It was a long way up. Hellishly long for a man out of shape and advancing in years. He wasn't the kid he had been. Breathing hard, he rounded the sixth and seventh landings, slowing down, the stink of cabbage and urine, what he thought of as prison smells, astringent in his nostrils. Up to the eighth, needing the handrail to propel himself on, and up and up again, every muscle in his legs burning.

When he finally reached the door, there was no response to his frantic knock.

He hammered on the glass.

No answer.

He tried the handle. The door was locked, but it didn't take him long to get inside. The tongue of the lock offered no real resistance when he put his shoulder to it.

The noise couldn't be helped; but if these people turned a blind eye to murder, they shouldn't be screaming at a little breaking and entering.

He moved through the squalid little flat, careful not to touch anything.

A kitchen, living room, bedroom, bathroom, all empty.

But at least there wasn't a corpse.

# TWENTY SEVEN

Frost watched as the man worked swiftly and efficiently, connecting the components for the last of the bombs. His hands moved with the fluency of a skilled mechanic, deft and confident. This wasn't someone who was fumbling his way through the assembly process. He'd done this before. More than once.

"Easy does it," O'Dwyer said, as he made the final connection and turned the screw on the terminal with the gentlest of touches. Frost had seen it done before, including a stint with the bomb squad when he first signed up with 1 Para, but never with real explosives. That had all been no more than blasting caps and detonators, not the full kit. He'd certainly never done anything like this on someone's dining table, a bottle of whiskey a couple of feet away.

"Now there, that wasn't so bad, was it?" O'Dwyer said. He looked at the clock. "Time to have that dram, I think."

Frost accepted the glass he was offered, raising it.

"*Sláinte*," O'Dwyer said, before emptying his own glass in a single mouthful.

Frost did the same, fighting back the cough that caught in his throat.

"That's enough for now," O'Dwyer said.

Con looking wistfully into his glass, the thin film of whiskey clinging to the side. He asked the question that Frost had been afraid to voice: "So, what's the plan?"

"Tomorrow," said O'Dwyer, "there's a special breakfast event in the restaurant at the top of the Midland Bank Tower, Canary Wharf. The PM, a couple of his Cabinet Ministers, a meet and greet for campaign fund donors."

Frost's mind was already racing.

The tower was already an iconic part of the London skyline, though not as immediately famous as other towers across the world; including the Post Office Tower, which had been a target of the IRA more than twenty years ago. That device had been found in the gents' toilets and dealt with before it could do any serious damage. But that was then. Both sides had learned a lot about guerrilla warfare during the intervening years.

"We've got a few of these bad boys," O'Dwyer said. "Tonight we rig them into the lift shaft and the emergency staircase."

"You're not planning on killing anyone?" Frost asked, surprised. The words were out of his mouth before the thought had finished forming inside his head.

"Lad, we don't need to kill to get our message across, and that's what counts. One voice. They'll hear us. They'll know what we could have done. That's what counts. That's how you frighten the crap out of these people. Actually killing them? That'd set the cause back a decade."

Frost nodded as if in agreement though he wasn't sure that he believed a word of what he was hearing. Had he been carrying a gun, right then, right there, he could have taken O'Dwyer down, taken control of the situation and shut it down. That wasn't an option. He needed to get a message in to Control somehow.

O'Dwyer began to carefully prepare everything for carrying out of the house. He saw the look on Frost's face. "Don't worry, Liam lad, they're not live yet," he laughed. "But don't drop 'em. The detonators would have your feet off."

Ten minutes later each of the bombs was stashed in the back of a battered old Ford that was parked outside. The street was empty. He couldn't see any sign of the security detail he'd hoped had tailed him there. Could be good, could be bad.

"You can drive," O'Dwyer said. "Just follow the van."

"What about you?"

"Oh, I'll be riding shotgun. Wouldn't expect you to do this on your own."

Frost's palms were already greased with sweat as he pulled away from the kerb, keeping close to the van.

The fact that O'Dwyer was travelling with him went a small way towards reassuring him the bombs wouldn't suddenly go off if he hit a pothole in the road.

He dried his hands on his jeans.

"No need to be nervous," O'Dwyer said. "We're on the side of the angels, Liam. It's a brave thing you're doing. A good thing. It *will* make a difference. That's what counts. Making a difference. But all the risks have been taken away. The only thing we need to worry about is not doing something stupid. By lunchtime tomorrow, the world will be a different. And that'll be because of us. You and me and soft lads like Con. Too many people have lost the stomach for the fight, taking the scraps from the English table and happy for them. That changes now."

Frost checked out the rear-view mirror as he drove. No sign of any headlights following him. There was no-one back there.

He was on his own.

# TWENTY EIGHT

Sir Charles gave directions from the A to Z that Terry had tucked in the glove compartment.

He found the Tube Station without too much difficulty, and after a couple of left hand turns, the road arced around to the right.

The street was a mixture of houses on the right, industry on the left.

"That's the old EMI factory up ahead," Terry said once he had slowed down sufficiently to be able to see a house number in the dark.

"This is probably close enough," Sir Charles said. "Pull over."

"Want me to come with you?"

"You armed?"

"Yes, Sir."

Sir Charles held his hand out.

"Can't do that, Sir." He was right, of course. A soldier on active duty couldn't possibly hand over his service weapon.

"You'd better come with me then," he relented.

The big man nodded.

Sir Charles took a deep breath then climbed out of the car.

There were lights on in several of the houses along the street, but no sign of anyone in the street itself. The large factory building loomed over the tarmac, casting its moonlight shadow. Maybe, once upon a time, it had been a thriving hotbed of industry; but now it was an empty shell.

He checked the numbers on the doors.

The house he was looking for was a dozen yards from where Terry had parked the car. The grubby lace curtains of the front room were barely visible through a deep vee where the thick velvet curtains hadn't quite drawn together. There was a ghost-light from a television playing inside the room.

He motioned for Terry to stand back before he knocked on the door.

A light went on in the hallway.

A shape shuffled towards the glass door.

The door opened after the rattle of a chain.

His stomach clenched tightly as he saw the woman in front of him, alive after all these years. His own, personal ghost.

"Greta," he said. Just that. Nothing else.

The years hadn't been kind to her. She was two years younger than he was, and looked twenty years older. The light behind her eyes had all but been extinguished. Where she had once been so full of life, there was only emptiness.

Seeing him, she said nothing; no hint that she even recognised him.

She just turned her back and shuffled back towards the television in the front room, leaving the door open for him to follow her. The rest of the house was in darkness and silent.

"Come in," he told Terry. "Check that the place is clear while I talk to Greta."

"You know her, then?"

"I used to," he said, then slipped into the front room, closing the door behind him.

"It's been a while," he said, perching on the arm of the sofa.

Greta lit a cigarette.

She didn't look away from the television set.

In the dim ghost-light of the screen, he could see the woman she had once been.

"Why didn't you get in touch?" he tried again, looking for a way into conversation, a way to ask all of those questions he wanted to ask. The problem was, opening that door, delving into their shared past, would only distract him from the point of his visit: Paddy O'Dwyer. He couldn't allow himself to be distracted. Frost was out there, alone.

She turned to look at him. A single glance.

"You left me there."

"There was no time," he said.

"Of course there was. You made a call. You left me to die. You could have got word to me. You didn't even try. Why should I come and find you, after that?"

Maybe she was right.

Maybe he could have done more.

Maybe he had only been worried about saving his own skin back then.

No: there were no maybes about it; he knew that. He'd always known it.

"I'm sorry," he said. It didn't seem like much, but it was all he had to offer.

"Sorry that you left me? Sorry that the Russians picked me up? Sorry that they raped and beat me? Sorry they burned my feet? Sorry they took me out every morning, put a blindfold on me and fired a rifle at the wall beside me? Sorry that I was on my knees night after night praying they would just kill me?"

"I'm sorry," he said again, knowing that it would never be adequate.

"Paddy came back for me," she said. "He traded my life. He came and got me out of the country. I'm only alive because of him. I owe him everything." She looked around at the room, as though to say, yes, this is everything: this bleak, damning, dispiriting everything.

"I had no idea."

"Of course you didn't. Why should you? I know all about your big, fancy house in the country. Paddy told me how you turned your back on him and just wanted to forget everything you had been through together. Must have been easy with all that money to wipe away your tears."

"That's not true," he said; but was he lying to her or to himself?

Had he really wanted to forget everything that had happed back then?

Yes. Of course. It had been the worst time of his life. Who would want to wallow in that? Prague had been the turning point. He'd known he wanted out, then; that he wasn't making a difference.

She shrugged. "What do you want?"

"Paddy?"

"He's not here."

"But he was, wasn't he?" She shrugged again. "Where has he gone?"

Another shrug.

He was going to press her again, push for a clue, when Terry knocked on the door.

"Come in."

The big man stuck his head inside the room.

Greta didn't take the slightest notice of him, turning her attention back to the television.

"I think you should take a look at this, sir," Terry said.

Sir Charles followed him into the back room, and saw the clutter of bits and pieces on the table. "A bomb factory," he said, looking at the remnants of wires and wrappings from the bomb caps and timing devices. Some of the components were crude—electrical tape and glaziers' putty—but the finished thing would be every bit as effective as Semtex, if it went off. It was an IRA special.

Terry nodded.

Sir Charles went back through to the lounge.

"Greta. I need you to tell me where he has gone."

There was a flash of anger in her eyes.

Even in the dim light there was no mistaking it.

"I don't betray my friends."

There was a moment of silence.

It was broken by the sound of a weapon being drawn.

Terry stood in the doorway.

He had his gun aimed at her face.

"I'm not afraid of dying," Greta said.

Terry tested the theory, walking right up beside her, pushing the black eye of the muzzle up against the middle of her forehead.

Greta Ciurak didn't blink. There were no tears. She didn't beg. She just stared through him at the television.

Sir Charles placed a hand on the young man's arm and shook his head.

When the threat of death holds no fear, there's nothing left.

She wasn't going to talk.

As if to emphasise the point, she said, "Kill me, Charley boy. Just finish what you started back in Prague. Kill me."

# TWENTY NINE

"She'll break," Terry said. "Take her in. She'll talk. Everyone does: you just need to find the right motivation."

"You weren't listening, were you?" asked Sir Charles. "After what the Russians did to her, nothing we do will break her. I won't be part of any torture. That's not the way I do things. And, before you argue, even if we could do it, she'll hold out long enough to make anything she does say useless, because we'll be watching the fallout on the news."

Terry was sceptical.

"What if she warns him?"

"He already knows I'm after him. He's not an idiot. He knows I've been brought in."

"How can you be sure?"

"Because someone in Five's using me to lure him out. They'll make sure he knows. I need to check in with Philip to see if he has had any joy."

"Surely he would have called if he'd found something?"

Sir Charles pulled out his phone, only to see that he had no signal.

He stepped out onto the roadside, his back to the house and the woman he'd loved once upon a time.

When he finally got a signal, there was a message from Philip waiting for him.

"I think I've found something," the voice said, and then broke off, hesitating. "I've been back into MI5's network. I don't know if this is anything, but there's one major event marked up for tomorrow. The PM's got a party gathering at the South Quay, first thing tomorrow. The Midland Bank Tower. I don't think I was supposed to be able to find it. The security protocol around it was off the charts: right up there with the stuff they had in the place when Rocket Ronnie came over. I took the liberty of checking surveillance around the tower. It's hard to tell from here, but it looks like someone has disabled part of the security. It's really hard to be sure, but in the coding, it looks like they've isolated one of the cameras. It could just be a fault, but, all things considered...I'm thinking, better safe than sorry."

"Canary Wharf," Sir Charles said, as Terry hustled around to the driver's side door, "the Midland Bank Tower."

He tried to call Philip back. He wanted to know what he meant about a higher level of security on the visit, and set him a new search to get to the root of who, exactly, was going to be at that morning meeting.

There was no reply.

They drove through the night faster than they should have done.

The car tripped every single speed camera between where they were and where they needed to be.

# THIRTY

The security guard at the front door was reluctant to open up.

Terry persuaded him. His attitude had nothing to do with the ID he flashed.

"What's the problem?" the guard asked.

"Security breach."

"Don't be ridiculous, I've been here all evening. Everything's fine. All quiet on the Western Front."

"And this the only way in?"

"Of course not. Look around you. There are a dozen emergency exits. But trust me: someone walks through one of those gates, an alarm would show up on my system. And I've got camera feeds on all of them. No alerts, no alarms, nothing on the CCTV."

"And that means nothing. Go and check outside," Sir Charles told Terry before he made his way around the desk to take a look at the grainy images flickering on the screens in the guard hut. He saw Terry's out-of-focus silhouette appear on the first screen, but while they waited for him to appear on the second, the image remained unchanged. They finally picked up Terry on the third screen.

The image on the middle screen remained static.

Someone had tampered with the camera feed, replacing the live feed with a static image.

"Is there an entrance there?" Sir Charles asked, rage bubbling just below the surface. What was the point of surrounding yourself with incompetent people?

The guard nodded.

"Show me."

Sir Charles followed the rent-a-cop around the perimeter only to see that Terry had already found his way inside.

This was more than just the case of a door being left open.

Philip was right to be concerned. Someone on the inside had set things up to allow them to get in and out without being noticed, covering their tracks with a faked video feed and circumventing the alarms on this door. With the Prime Minister being due inside the building in less than twelve hours, the place was a security nightmare. There was construction going on all over the Wharf, with the ground being cleared for a major tower that would, when finished, be one of the tallest in the country.

"We need to a full sweep of the building," he told Terry. "Now."

"Agreed. But we can't do that alone. This place is huge. We need back-up."

"There's no time for that. We've got to use our heads. Where's O'Dwyer likely to hit? He won't bomb indiscriminately, it's not his style; so what's his target within the complex?" Sir Charles answered his own question. "There's an observation area on the top floor, which they're turning into a restaurant for the morning. That's where the meeting's happening." He turned to the guard. "Go back to your post. Call the police if you haven't heard from us in fifteen minutes."

The guard nodded.

He looked lost.

Sir Charles knew that he hadn't signed up for this kind of thing, no matter that the threat of IRA action hung over the city at all times. That was the cost of living in the capital.

They entered the building together.

"I'll take the lift," Sir Charles told Terry. "I want you to take the stairs. Look for anything out of place. Any sign that someone's been in there. And for Christ's sake, be thorough. We can't afford to miss a thing."

Terry reached around and pulled a 9mm from the waistband of his trousers. "Take this," he said, then opened his jacket to reveal his own weapon. "It's my backup."

Sir Charles nodded, and racked the slide.

He headed across the deserted foyer for the lift.

It was ready and waiting for him.

He stepped inside and pushed the button for the restaurant.

He was banking on the fact that O'Dwyer wouldn't shoot before seeing who it was stepping out.

It was a risk.

It wasn't like he knew his old partner's state of mind.

He didn't know the man at all; that much was obvious.

Yet how could O'Dwyer have changed so much that he genuinely saw bombs, death and absolute devastation as a viable means to action? Those were the tools of terror. The weapons of last resort. They'd fought side-by-side against the kinds of regimes that saw terror as a genuine recourse.

How could it have come to this?

The ride to the top floor gave Sir Charles the time to think: something that they had never had in the old days.

Everything had happened so quickly. They'd been working on instinct and relying on their training.

That, he realised, was so much better than the alternative.

Time was a destroyer.

He closed his eyes.

The elevator chimed.

The doors opened.

He stood in the doorway, waiting for the bullets to hit.

He was almost disappointed when they didn't.

There was no-one there.

# THIRTY ONE

The blow had come hard and fast before the world had gone dark for Frost.

O'Dwyer had lulled him with all of his faux-camaraderie. Frost hadn't seen it coming. They had driven through the deserted streets of Canary Wharf, angling through the turns, skirting the building site and the towering cranes towards South Quay, and pulled up in the dark space between deluxe apartment complexes and the sleek glass towers of new bank buildings. They'd crossed the street fast, heads down, and found security gates open and a door at the back of the tower unlocked. They'd moved quickly, carrying the homemade bombs inside.

The men in the van had helped, but once they were inside it was just O'Dwyer and Frost. Con had stayed in the van the whole time, while the fourth man, Lorcan Kelly, moved it out of sight.

They carried two of the bombs to the top of the tower.

Frost set his down, and as he straightened, he felt something slam brutally into the back of his head. His legs crumpled beneath him, his entire body stiffening as he went down, unable to stop himself.

And then there was nothing.

He had no idea how long he'd been out. Seconds. Minutes.

He opened his eyes to see that he'd been propped up against a wall, hands tied behind his back. It took a moment to realise that he was sitting at the top of a flight of stairs.

He felt a weight on his chest.

He looked down, knowing what it was already.

The second makeshift bomb had been taped to his chest.

"Welcome back, you cunt," said O'Dwyer.

"What the fuck are you doing, man?" Frost asked.

"Cut the bullshit. I know you're a fucking plant. I can smell it all over you. You might be able to fool idiots like Con, but I've been around the block. I was you before you, and I'll always be a bigger cunt than you could ever imagine."

"What the fuck are you talking about, man?" His denial was rewarded with a slap that had his head ringing.

"I know that you're MI5. Just like those two amateurs who were sitting in the car, watching your flat."

There was nothing to be gained from denying it again. He'd been made. It was over. Now it was all about trying to get out of this alive.

"What have you done with them?"

"I ended them," he said. Simple as that.

"So what now?"

"Now? Now, I finish planting the rest of the bombs, and we make us some noise."

"You're off your head. There's no way this is happening. It isn't going to end the way you want. They know what you're doing. They're onto you. It's already over. You just don't know it yet."

"I don't hear any fucking sirens. No-one's looking for you here. You're fucked, you little shite. And before you get any ideas about trying to tear that bomb vest off, think about this:

mercury switch. You know what that is, right? Any sudden movements and you're fucked, you fucking fucker. Ba-boom."

"Then I take you with me."

O'Dwyer tore a strip of gaffer tape of a roll and pressed it over Frost's mouth, silencing him.

"Too much noise. I can't think."

He got to his feet and left Frost to think about his future, however short it might be.

The door closed behind him, plunging the stairwell into darkness.

Any thought Frost might have harboured about trying to extricate himself from the bomb vest evaporated as soon as the lights went out. Unable to see, there was no way he was trying to wriggle out of it and risking tripping the switch.

# THIRTY TWO

The impromptu restaurant was deserted, the skeletal outlines of the chairs creating a nightmarish landscape in front of him.

The tables were already laid out, Charles realised: silver service, ready for the gathering. There was no sign of a living soul.

They were too late.

O'Dwyer had already been and gone.

Which meant the explosives were in place.

He scanned the room. There was nothing obviously wrong, but of course, it wouldn't be. Paddy O'Dwyer had gone through the same training he had. He knew rudimentary demolitions stuff; most army boys did.

He needed to call it in to the bomb squad.

Every second counted.

The alternative was that he was completely wrong. That this wasn't the target. That O'Dwyer had led him here by the nose because he knew who was sniffing after him and knew exactly what would get him interested.

Holding the gun out in front of him, he started to make his way around the room.

There had to be something out of place.

Something wrong.

The place settings were done with precision, each piece of cutlery perfectly aligned. Something wrong should be noticeably wrong. It should stand out. The night beyond the windows was black, save for the winking wing lights of a plane coming in to London City airport.

The sound of a door opening and closing broke the silence.

He pressed himself back against the wall.

Even as fit as he was, Terry couldn't have made it all the way to the top in such a short space of time, which meant it had to be someone else. And that meant it had to be O'Dwyer, or one of his crew.

The darkness might still offer the element of surprise if the Irishman didn't know Sir Charles was in there.

He held his breath and listened to the sound of his heart, loud in his ears.

It had been too long since he had felt like this; too long since the surge of adrenalin had been the only thing that could make him feel truly alive.

Another door opened.

A figure stepped through, carrying a box.

He recognised him across the years, despite the darkness: Paddy O'Dwyer.

He had changed, and yet he was in so many ways exactly the same.

Sir Charles didn't move.

He watched his old partner place the battered cardboard box on the floor beside a heating vent, handling it with exaggerated care, and knew exactly what was inside.

On his knees, O'Dwyer pulled a screwdriver from his pocket.

"Hello Paddy," Sir Charles said. "It's been a long time."

The pause was no more than a heartbeat, O'Dwyer still on his knees, twisting around to find the source of the voice, followed by the instant of recognition. "Charley! I wish I could say it was a pleasure, but I always knew you'd find me. Can't let you stop me, though. You understand that, don't you?"

"This isn't you, Paddy."

"Oh, it is. It really is." Then he rose slowly, pushing himself up onto his feet, screwdriver still in hand. His gaze drifted toward the doorway he'd come in through. "I take it the rat in the stairwell is one of yours? You really should try harder. He wasn't right. You can tell when someone's a believer. He might have said the right things, even done the right things, but he wasn't a believer. How did you do it? With the guy in the hospital? A bait and switch? Come on, you can tell me. Because there's no way you'd let one of yours pull the trigger. You're supposed to be the good guys. Honour. Integrity. You play by the rules."

"There are no rules. He pulled the trigger," Sir Charles said, though it was very much a case of shades of truth.

"No fucking way! You're kidding me. You let that shit-for-brains kill an innocent man, just to maintain his cover? I'm impressed, Charley. That's fucking dark. Good for you. You grew a pair of balls."

"Is he dead?"

"Where would be the fun in that?"

"That's good, that's very good. We can all walk away from this, then. Nobody else gets hurt."

O'Dwyer shook his head. "Too late for that, Charley. Promises made. Promises have got to be kept. I'm a man of my word. A man of principles. If you ain't got your honour, what have you got?"

"You're not a terrorist, Paddy."

"No, you're right, I'm not. Never have been. Never will be. You know why? Because I'm fighting for something I *believe*

**180**

in. This is from the heart. This is righteous. I'm on the side of the angels, no matter what you think. I ain't a terrorist. I'm a freedom fighter, Charley. That's more than just semantics. You know, I always dreamed this day would come, you and me: the old band back together. Can't say this was how I imagined it'd go down, you holding a gun to my head. Doesn't feel right. You remember Prague?"

"Of course I do."

"You remember what happened there, when we were trying to get out? I saved your life, Charley. In some cultures, that means I'm responsible for it. Your life is in my hands."

"Doesn't look that way at the moment, does it?" Sir Charles looked down at the gun in his hand.

"Looks can be deceptive, Charley. Fact is you owe me. And not just a little bit. You owe me your life. That's huge, Charley. That's a debt that can't be repaid."

"I can't let you do this, Paddy."

"In that case, you're going to have to shoot me, old friend. And if you ask me that would seem like a piss-poor way of paying me back. And you know, in the interests of clearing the air, I always knew about your crush on Greta; but I didn't do anything about it. I didn't want to compromise the mission. I let you carry your torch. But it wasn't you who went back for her, was it? You hiked cross-country, and got the fuck out of there. As soon as you were safe, I turned right around and went back. I got her out, Charley. I got Greta out. You might think you loved her, but you didn't. If you had, there is no way you could have left her. You'd have done what I did. You'd have turned right around and gone back to save her."

"I've seen her," Sir Charles said.

"Of course you have. You were meant to."

"She didn't tell me where you were."

"And you didn't beat it out of her? I'm disappointed in you, Charley."

"That's not my style."

"Of course it's your style. You're not some innocent. You might like to think of yourself that way, but you've got blood on your hands. You and the people you work for. Blood all over your grubby little hands."

"You're wrong," Sir Charles said, though it was impossible not to wonder if, deep down, somewhere in his heart-of-hearts, Paddy wasn't at least a little bit right. It was all words, wasn't it? Liberator, freedom fighter, terrorist, oppressor, rebel, hero; all just words, spinning one form of truth over another, depending on who emerged victorious.

"So what side are you on then, Charley? Freedom or Oppression?" O'Dwyer asked, making it sound so black and white. It could never be. It was such a big question. One better men than they were had wrestled with, and failed to answer. One steeped in blood as far back as the days of Oliver Cromwell and the bloody murders of Drogheda, only reinforced by the Easter Rising and the War of Independence. So many broken promises and broken truces. There was no easy answer. No quick solution.

"Don't do this, Paddy. It doesn't have to end this way."

"It won't end here tonight, Charley. This is bigger than you and me and our personal story. This is one for the history books. When this bomb goes off, it'll change everything. Let me tell you a secret: I've finally found something that's worth dying for, Charley."

"Don't make me pull the trigger, Paddy. Don't make me do this," Sir Charles said, raising the gun, prepared to kill his old friend if he had to.

"Drop the weapon, Sir Charles," a voice said calmly in his ear. A moment later, he felt the muzzle of a gun pressed into his back. "It won't help you. It's empty anyway."

"Terry?"

Sir Charles judged the weight of the weapon in his hand. It felt right. Meaning he'd switched the live rounds out for blanks. That, or he was bluffing. That was always a possibility. He could pull the trigger and find out easily enough if he'd been taken in by a wolf in sheep's clothing. He was ring-rusty. He'd been out of the field too long. Much too long.

"Sit down, please," said Terry. "I just need to talk to O'Dwyer. No-one's going to get hurt. It's over now." He was incredibly calm. "I need you to focus on me, Patrick. Listen. I've got a message from Control. It's time to come in from the cold, soldier. I've been sent to bring you in. You've done good. Really good. There's a medal in this for you, but it's over now. It's time to come home."

There was a moment of confusion, Sir Charles racing to catch up, finally understanding.

"I'm not going anywhere with you," O'Dwyer said. His knuckles were white around the screwdriver's handle.

It had all been nothing but shadow play.

The problem was, O'Dwyer had forgotten he was an actor, and had lost himself in the part. The bombs, however, were very real. He was sure of that.

Terry took a step towards O'Dwyer, hand out, as though trying to calm a rabid dog. The gesture was about as pointless. O'Dwyer was fast. Faster than Terry Saines could have imagined. And he'd turned.

O'Dwyer took two steps towards the big man, then stepped inside his reach, twisted, and rammed the blade of the screwdriver into his neck.

There was no coming back from that.

It was only the fact that the screwdriver was still in O'Dwyer's hand that stopped Terry from going down. He was already dead, it was just taking a couple of seconds for the message to pass from his heart to his brain and shut things down.

"I'm going to give you a chance, Charley," O'Dwyer said, "for old time's sake. Because your life is mine to do with as I chose. I'm going to let you go now. Walk out of here. Do not pass Go. Do not collect two hundred pounds. Liam—or whatever the fuck he's really called—is in the stairwell with a bomb vest taped to his chest. Get him out of here. Let me do this."

"I can't let you kill anyone else, Paddy," Sir Charles said.

O'Dwyer shook his head. "I'm not going to. This isn't about killing. It's about the message. It's about the world knowing we're still here; we're still fighting. It's about my country, Charley. It's about freedom. Self rule. It's about getting the troops off our streets. It's about making the old country beauty-fucking-ful again. A place where Irishmen aren't killing Irishmen, where it isn't about loyalist and republicans. A place where which version of the same god you worship isn't going to get you killed. Where you don't grow up as a kid with a Molotov cocktail in your hand, chasing down army transports. Where kids in school aren't thinking they're at war because they can't walk down the street. It's about everything, Charley. You can't understand. You just can't, because you're not one of us. So go. Go with my blessing. Find Greta if you want. Go back to her and make amends. Try and convince her to forgive you. Maybe this time, she'll love you back."

"What are you going to do, Paddy?"

"I'm going to do what I came here to do. I'm going to die."

# THIRTY THREE

But it could never be as simple as that.

"I can't let you do that, Paddy. You're not this man. You're a legend. You're a story. You're not a terrorist. The cloak you've been wearing to hide yourself amongst the IRA—that's not who you are. They want to bring you home."

"Patrick O'Dwyer is dead, Charley. He's been dead for years."

Sir Charles shook his head. "Don't do this."

"You really want to help me? You really want to save me? Is that it? Is this your way of paying back your guilt? Save me now to make up for me saving you in Prague? Then we're even? Is that how your mind's working? Because I don't want to be saved. I really don't. There's nothing to save me from."

"Come home with me, Paddy." He held out his hand. "It can be just like old times. You and me again."

And for a moment, it looked as though he was getting through to the Irishman.

It was in his eyes.

Regret.

Sadness.

Understanding.

O'Dwyer stepped towards him, closing the gap.

And rammed the screwdriver, still slick with another man's blood, into Sir Charles' stomach, opening him up.

O'Dwyer pulled the screwdriver out, and then rammed it in again, opening another hole in Sir Charles's body.

Then again.

His side. His chest.

Sir Charles felt the metal scrape against the bones of his ribs, looking for his heart.

The sudden flare of pain was agonising.

Every nerve and fibre screamed as one.

His hand clamped over the handle of the screwdriver—over O'Dwyer's hand—holding it in, desperately trying to stem the flow of blood. His legs betrayed him. His head swam. He clung stubbornly to consciousness. But it was hard. So hard. The world struggled to turn to black all around him.

"You always were too trusting, Charley."

# THIRTY FOUR

He couldn't stop him.

He couldn't follow him.

He crawled towards the doorway, leaving a slick of blood behind him.

His vision came and went.

He called out, "Frost?" But had no idea if his voice would carry—if he'd even managed to say it aloud.

O'Dwyer was gone.

So was the bomb.

He dragged himself on a few more precious, agonising feet.

He tried to stand, but couldn't. His entire body folded under him.

He cried out again. Heard something in return. A voice?

"Frost? Help me."

There was a muffled sound coming from below, but the blood in his ears and the screaming pain inside his head drowned out any real words that might have been said.

"Frost," he called out again, his hands slick with blood as he crawled towards the door.

He reached out, pushing at the bottom of the door.

There was some sort of sensor; it opened by itself.

He dragged himself out into the stairwell.

It was pitch dark.

Until it wasn't.

Motion sensors.

The lights came on above his head, throwing the stairwell into stark relief.

He could see Frost leaning against the wall, the bulky shape of the makeshift bomb taped to his chest. Frost looked up at him. The soldier had electrical tape across his mouth.

He wasn't moving.

Sir Charles slumped down across the first step, a red tide spilling down over the edge. He pushed himself on, then started to fall forward, and couldn't stop his weight taking him down.

He tumbled down the eight short steps to the landing where Frost sat.

Fear blazed in the other man's eyes.

Sir Charles realised how close he'd come to slumping into his side.

Using the wall, and summoning every last ounce of strength he had, he pushed himself up, one hand on the floor, the other, trembling, reaching out to tear the tape from Frost's mouth.

He couldn't free the ties that bound him.

"Mercury switch," Frost gasped, and Sir Charles understood the fear.

He'd come a couple of inches from blowing them both to kingdom come.

"I can't...I don't...I'm...sorry."

"Can you get my hands free?"

"I can't..."

"Then we're both going to die here."

# THIRTY FIVE

Frost risked an inch, no more, just edging slightly around so that part of his arm was away from the wall.

"Can you reach where I'm tied?"

"No."

He swallowed.

Sweat broke out on his skin and ran down over the ridge at the base of his neck.

The man beside him was in a bad way. Blood pooled around where he sat slumped up against the wall. He had multiple stab wounds. His skin was the grey of putty. If he didn't get help soon, he wouldn't get out of this place.

Then again, it wasn't like his own prospects were so much better.

"What's your name?" Frost said, trying to engage the older man, get him talking, concentrating: get him focused on living.

"Charles."

"That's good. Hello, Charles. I need you to stay with me, Charles." Repeat his name, turn it into a mantra. "Because you and me, we're getting out of this place, and the only way we can do that is together."

"I can't..."

"No such thing, Charles. You're better than can't. You have to be. I can't do this alone. I need to get my hands free. If we just concentrate on that one small thing, that's not so much. If we can do that, we can do anything. So let's just focus on my hands. Okay?"

The other man was fading fast. He'd lost a phenomenal amount of blood. But he was stubborn. He reached out with a trembling hand for Frost's wrists where the tape bound him. Frost tried to edge another couple of inches around so that more of his back was turned towards the Five man.

"That's good, Charles. That's really good. You can do this. Just concentrate on my hands."

He could only pray that O'Dwyer hadn't done a great job at fixing down the edges of the tape, so Charles could get a decent grip to unwind it.

"I can't risk moving too much, Charles, or I'd help you. But if this thing goes, we're fucked. So I need you to be strong. Can you do that for me? Can you be strong?" He couldn't see the other man's face now. "Help me, and I'll help you. I'll carry you out of this place. I'll get you to a hospital. You'll be all right. All you need to do is stay with me."

He felt a tug at the tape, followed by another, and the sound of the glue peeling away. The third tug released some of the tension around his wrists, giving him some wiggle room. He began to slowly work his hands loose, barely daring to breathe for fear of tripping the mercury switch. He could almost feel the bomb ticking away against his body, waiting to explode.

And then his hands were free.

He still couldn't risk moving properly; nothing had changed, really.

The older man slumped back beside him, his breathing becoming a wet rattle against his lips. Not good.

There wasn't a hope in hell of defusing the bomb. The best he could hope was to get it off without triggering the tilt switch. He couldn't tell if it was armed. He didn't know enough about O'Dwyer to know if the man was a psycho, or if he really did see himself as a modern day Michael Collins. Psychologically, the bomb itself was enough to take Frost out of the game, primed or not. With no way of knowing, he was never going to risk trying to lift it off over his head, just in case he gambled wrong.

"Are you still with me, Charles?"

Nothing.

"Charles? Talk to me, Charles."

Nothing.

"Damn you, Charley, talk to me."

"Yes." It was only a word, but it was better than nothing.

"I need you to do something else for me, Charley. I need you to look at the bomb on my chest and see if you can tell if it's live. Can you do that? You don't need to do anything demanding, just look."

Tentatively, Frost edged round. Just a fraction at a time. "Look at the wires, can you see if they're connected? Is the circuit complete?"

"I don't...I can't see."

"You can do this, Charley. You can do this. Look."

"No."

"You can do this."

"No."

"Charley!"

"No...loose...wire."

Frost closed his eyes.

He let out a slow breath.

"Are you sure, Charley?"

"Yes."

"Because if you're wrong, we're both getting blown up," Frost said, managing to sound almost cheerful.

"Funny."

"I am. You'll learn to love that about me, Charley."

"Charles. Not. Charley."

"Sure. I'll call you whatever you want, just stick with me. Okay, Charles? We're in this together."

Frost started working at the tape where it held the bomb to his chest. His hands slipped, and for a moment he thought he'd fucked up well and truly, because he heard a click from somewhere down by his chest.

But the bomb didn't blow.

"I guess you were right, Charles."

"Always am."

"Ah, well, that's good to know. So, I'm going to get this off, and then I'm going to carry you out of here. We've done the hard part now, Charles. Now it's all about staying alive. You can do that."

He heard footsteps above him and realised that O'Dwyer must have gone towards the roof to plant his final device.

He moved quickly, still very much aware that the detonator would pack enough punch to do some serious damage to the pair of them if he got it wrong.

After he'd loosened the last band of tape, Frost took hold of the bomb with both hands, easing it away from his chest. He kept his eyes fixed on the box, trying to ensure that none of the components became dislodged as he slowly lifted it away, just a fraction of an inch at a time, and lowered it.

Frost set the bomb down on the concrete stair and stared at it.

"Go," Charles said.

"Not without you, Charles. We have a deal."

"No. I won't...make it. Go. Get O'Dwyer. You have to. Stop him. He's not...who he was."

He heard movement above.

The elevator.

"Stop him."

Frost pushed himself to his feet, trapped in indecision.

"That's...an order. Soldier."

"Yes, sir. You stay here, Charles. Promise me. I'll be back. When this is done, I'll be back to get you out."

"I can't promise that," Charles said.

Frost started running, taking the steps too fast, three and four and even five at a time, jumping down to the next landing, hitting the floor hard and running even as he landed. The sheer speed of his descent almost sent him tumbling down the stairs.

As he reached the next landing, he felt the air sucked out of the stairwell in a huge upwards drag, followed a second later by an ear-splitting explosion that ripped the world apart.

Plaster rained down from above, followed by brick and twisted metal, chased by fire.

It wasn't close enough for it to have come from the bomb that had been strapped to his chest; it had to be from up above, the bomb up on the observation platform.

Charles was alive or he wasn't. It was as simple as that. He was Schrödinger's Operative: alive and dead at the same time, until proven otherwise. Frost was going to have to live with that. Charles had been right: O'Dwyer had to be stopped. Even so, he stood on the stairs, staring up at the smoke and rock dust swelling down the shaft, thinking about charging back up there to where the older man lay.

Frost had barely registered the thought, when his whole world seemed to be ripped apart, and he was falling as the guts of the stairwell collapsed.

The ceiling above Frost came down.

A huge chunk of masonry crashed to the stairs behind him.

Frost didn't slow down.

He couldn't.

Slowing down meant being crushed to death. And he'd made a promise.

One thing Ronan Frost learned about himself in those few terrifying seconds, as smoke filled his lungs, as he stumbled, falling, was that he was a man of his word.

# THIRTY SIX

The room was painfully reminiscent of the one where he'd watched Frost pump bullets into a corpse.

He had no idea of how long ago that had been.

The machine beside him repeated its relentless *beep, beep, beep*. It wasn't as reassuring as it should have been.

It had taken rescue workers hours to free him from the rubble.

He was lucky.

Incredibly lucky.

He'd been unconscious when the first bomb up in the observation area detonated. The bomb disposal team said it had been triggered by remote. The second one, close to him, had never gone off. That was the difference between life and death. The ceiling and wall had come down around him, forming a pocket of air that kept him alive long enough for the rescue workers to dig him out, and protected him from the worst of the collapse. O'Dwyer had planted three other devices in the tower, but like the one he'd strapped to Frost's chest, none of them had been primed.

There were shades of lucky.

The doctors had looked him in the eye and told him he was a lucky man. He'd survived the systemic shock of the stabbing, the blood loss and the bomb blast.

In the next breath they said that the subsequent collapse had damaged his spine, severing the spinal cord, and that he would never walk again.

There were definitely shades of lucky.

He was angry.

Angry at Five, at Paddy O'Dwyer, at himself. Angry at the world.

He'd seen reports on the small television in the corner of the room: the bombing had caused very little damage to the tower itself, the only casualty an unnamed British soldier. It wouldn't derail the peace process, which was O'Dwyer's sole aim. A second bomb had gone off outside at 19:01 the following evening, a truck bomb containing 500kg of ammonium nitrate fertilizer and sugar, directly under the railway line where the tracks crossed Marsh Wall. A warning call 90 minutes beforehand had saved thousands of lives. Even so, Inan Bashir and John Jeffries, two men working in the local newsagents, hadn't been evacuated in time. There were 39 other injuries.

It could have been so much worse.

He knew that.

He'd had a middle-of-the-night visit from Ronan Frost. He had still been half out of his mind with the morphine pulsing through his system, so it could have been a drug-dream. He couldn't remember much about the visit, only that he'd told the Irishman that O'Dwyer had saved his life, and that it had been a mistake. He meant that he would have rather died back there in Prague than like this, a slow, lingering collapse, but that wasn't how the Irishman had taken it.

One of the suits from MI5 had visited, during one of his more lucid days, and introduced himself as Quentin Carruthers. He was an effeminate man, immaculately dressed, with long, delicate fingers that seemed freakishly long as they formed a tent beneath his chin. "They'll want a full report from you, of course," Carruthers said, eventually.

"Good thing that I didn't lose the use of my hands as well, then."

"Now, now, Charles old chap; that's hardly the spirit, is it?"

"What do you want from me?"

"Despite all appearances, I'd say you actually did quite well back there, Charles. You're too good to turn your back on this life."

"I couldn't turn my back if I wanted to."

"You really do have quite an acerbic tongue on you, don't you, Charley?"

"Don't you *ever* call me that."

"Apologies, *Sir* Charles. Like it or not, your country needs men like you. You were made for this life."

"You can hardly recall me to active duty. Haven't you heard? I'm never going to walk again."

"You don't need to. Not for what I have in mind. All that running about is a young man's game. We need someone like you, someone who can do things we can't, who can get dirty when our hands are tied."

"You mean deniable." It was a statement, not a question.

The man smiled and nodded.

"Think about it. Your own team, all the resources you could want. Remit to go places we can't go. You'll be able to really make a difference. And that's all any of us can want, isn't it? That's why we get into this: out of a fierce patriotic desire to make a difference. Being in a chair doesn't have to end your life, Sir Charles. I know what sort of man you are."

"If I do this, I'm going to want Frost," he said, already thinking about it. "And autonomy. I need to pick my own team. Answer to no one. I can't be dragging into the city every day. I want to run this from Nonesuch."

"That was our way of thinking, too. Build your own team. Take your time; recruit the right people. There's no hurry. I'll be your point of contact inside the Service." Meaning he'd be Control. "Frost's due to report back to 1 Para in a couple of days, though he's expressed an interest with joining the SAS counter-terrorist unit. I think it could be very good for him. Broaden his world view." Which meant, get him away from the ideologies of Ireland and the Troubles of his native land. They'd already lost one good man to it in O'Dwyer. That was the risk of going under deep cover. Sometimes an agent lost his grip on who he really was outside of his legend. Sometimes he started to genuinely share the sympathies of his fictional alter ego. For Patrick O'Dwyer, the lines had blurred. They couldn't allow that to happen to another good man.

"Let me think about it."

"Take your time."

He would. Time was the one thing he had in abundance.

# EPILOGUE

Ronan Frost followed a man into Malone's, a bar in Holborn.

The barman, towelling out a pint glass, nodded to him as he approached the bar.

He paid his money.

As the barman put his glass down to take it, he said, "Didn't expect to see you in here again, Liam."

"Unfinished business," Frost told him. He saw Con O'Toole propping up the fruit machine in the corner of the snug, a cigarette perched on the side of the machine beside his half-empty pint glass. "Put one in the pipe for Con."

"You sure this is wise, Liam? You're not exactly welcome around here at the moment."

"My name's not Liam."

"None of my business. I don't want any trouble."

"Bit late for that. This is the way it's going to happen: you're going to empty this place. Then you're going to make a call. You're going to summon Paddy O'Dwyer, I don't care what you tell him, just get him here. And don't try and tell me you don't know how to reach him. You know. You've been harbouring these guys for a couple of years now, we know all about you. So if you don't want to lose your nice little number here, you'll do as you're told. I'm just going to sit quietly in the corner with my pint and wait for O'Dwyer to arrive."

"What are you going to do?"

"I told you, I'm going to have my drink."

"That's not what I meant."

"You don't want to know. Just do your part. Make the call. Get Paddy here."

Frost watched the man make the call.

He was a good liar.

When he hung up, the barman looked at the young Irishman. "I can't be here for this."

"Then go. I'm not stopping you. This is going to happen. It has to."

The barman nodded. He gathered his things together and gave Frost the keys.

"Lock up after you."

He put up a sign in the window that said closed, and slammed home the bolt in the top of the door that would stop anyone wandering in from the street.

Frost dealt with Con next. "Answer a question for me, Con."

The drunk looked sober for the first time in a decade. "What do you want? Fucking traitor."

"Do you want to die here?"

"What kind of question is that?"

"I'm serious Con. This isn't about you. I don't want to kill you, but if you won't do as I tell you, if I can't trust you to do it, it's just going to be much easier for me if you're not around."

"You're serious? Fuck…"

"In a few minutes, Paddy's going to come banging on that door. You're going to let him in."

"What are you going to do?"

"I'm going to end him, Con."

"Fuck."

"Breathe a word, and you go, too. Try to warn him, light's out."

"Fuck. Who the fuck are you?"

"I'm the devil, Con. You're a God-fearing man. Can't you tell?"

"Fuck. Just fuck."

"When Paddy gets here, you've got one job: you've got to get him into the office. Can you do that?" Frost nodded towards the door with the stick man painted on it.

Con nodded.

"Good. I'll take care of everything else. Don't disappoint me, Con. Believe me, I don't deal with disappointment well."

"You can trust me, Liam. We're good. Pie and pint, right? We're good."

"I hope so, Con. I truly hope so."

"Fuck," the old drunk shook his head again.

It took another forty minutes before Paddy O'Dwyer came banging on the glass. Forty minutes for Con O'Toole to lose his nerve or grow some balls. Frost wasn't hopeful.

He waited in the stall. The place reeked of piss. It turned his stomach. The porcelain urinals hadn't been cleaned out in a month. They were thick with yellow-stained grime.

He could hear them outside the bathroom, talking. O'Dwyer demanding to know what was going on, where the barman was, Con telling him he didn't know, only that he'd been summoned, too, and that Lorcan Kelly was on his way. O'Dwyer grunted. Told Con to pull them a couple of pints, he was off for a piss.

The bathroom door opened.

Frost watched Paddy O'Dwyer step up to the stall, waited until he heard the man unzip and knew he had his cock in his

**201**

hand, mid-stream, before he stepped up behind him, grabbed a tangle of hair and slammed his face forward into the filthy tiles.

Paddy's piss went everywhere, streaming high as his legs went from under him.

Frost grabbed his head again and slammed his face into the lip of the porcelain urinal again and again until his hands came away bloody, then he let the IRA man collapse into the pool of his own piss and stood over him.

He drew his gun, his service piece, not the one he'd used to put two shots into a dead man a few days ago, and said, "A message from Charles. You should never have saved his life."

Frost pulled the trigger.

# THE END

# THE OGMIOS DIRECTIVE

## Crucible

Steven Savile & Steve Lockley

## Solomon's Seal

Steven Savile & Steve Lockley

## Lucifer's Machine

Steven Savile & Rick Chesler

## Wargod

Steven Savile & Sean Ellis

## Shining Ones

Steven Savile & Richard Salter

## Argo

Steven Savile & Ashley Knight

Lightning Source UK Ltd.
Milton Keynes UK
UKHW02f2036210218
318287UK00004B/280/P